Yonder

The fifth volume in
a collection of writings by

C.J.S. Hayward

C.J.S. Hayward Publications, Wheaton

1. Feminism, Biblical Egalitarianism, and complementarianism. 2. Feminism and political correctness. 3. Men and women. 4. Gender roles. 5. Christianity and sexuality. 6. Embodiment and disembodiment--fiction. 7. Science fiction.

ISBN 978-0-6152-0217-4

The reader is invited to visit CJSHayward.com.

Contents

Inclusive Language Greek Manuscript Discovered

MINNEAPOLIS (AP) -- There is a considerable buzz among New Testament scholars over the discovery of a near-complete Greek manuscript to the book of the Bible called Romans. The manuscript is similar to others, but is the first known manuscript to mirror the *Today's New International Version* (TNIV) in its use of inclusive language.

There is a wide consensus among both conservative and liberal scholars that most Greek manuscripts use grammatically masculine words where the original author meant to include women as fully as men. This manuscript, referred to by scholars as R221819, is similar to other such manuscripts but uses inclusive language where applicable.

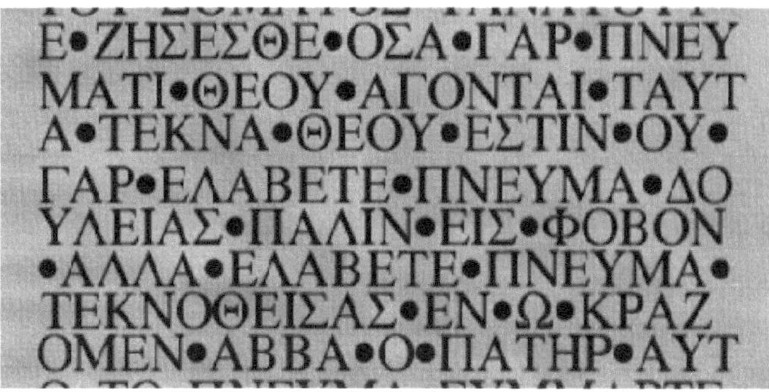

Ε•ΖΗΣΕΣΘΕ•ΟΣΑ•ΓΑΡ•ΠΝΕΥ
ΜΑΤΙ•ΘΕΟΥ•ΑΓΟΝΤΑΙ•ΤΑΥΤ
Α•ΤΕΚΝΑ•ΘΕΟΥ•ΕΣΤΙΝ•ΟΥ•
ΓΑΡ•ΕΛΑΒΕΤΕ•ΠΝΕΥΜΑ•ΔΟ
ΥΛΕΙΑΣ•ΠΑΛΙΝ•ΕΙΣ•ΦΟΒΟΝ
•ΑΛΛΑ•ΕΛΑΒΕΤΕ•ΠΝΕΥΜΑ•
ΤΕΚΝΟΘΕΙΣΑΣ•ΕΝ•Ω•ΚΡΑΖ
ΟΜΕΝ•ΑΒΒΑ•Ο•ΠΑΤΗΡ•ΑΥΤ

A portion of R221819, containing Romans 8:14-15

The book of Romans was first written in Greek and is considered foundational in its treatment of what it means to be a Christian. Chapter eight is well-known among people who read the Bible; its fourteenth and fifteenth verses are shown above. *Huioi* ("sons") in verse 14 is replaced by a more inclusive *tekna* ("children"), and various word forms are adapted to a gender-neutral spelling. R221819 is thought to reflect the TNIV's distinguishing features with considerable accuracy.

Kenneth Barker, one of the leading scholars involved with the TNIV, said, "I don't think this is quite as big of a deal as people make. It's just a minor change, like other textual variations, and simply clarifies the author's intent." He disclaims any greater significance to the discovery.

The progressive element of Christians for Biblical Equality has been jubilant. One scholar said, "This is a very important step in the right direction. I look forward to when a manuscript is found where the patriarchal *Theos* is replaced by the more neutral *Theon*. It really only means changing a couple of the case endings plus the spelling of the word that means 'the.' *Theon* would remain in the second declension. It is just a small change, but it would help Christians reach out effectively to those on the margins of society." After all, if one clarification helps, why not another?

Knights and Ladies

I would like to talk about men and women and the debate about whether we are genuinely different or whether this aspect of our bodies is just packaging that has no bearing on who we are. I would like to begin by talking about three things:

- "Egalitarianism," which says not only that men and women are due equal respect but the differences are differences of body only and not differences of mind, heart, and spirit.
- "Complementarianism," which says that there are real and personal differences, and men and women are meant to complement each other.
- Why the debate between egalitarianism and complementarianism is like a car crash.

Egalitarianism, Complementarianism, and Car Crashes

I was in a theology class when the professor argued emphatically that for two claims to contradict each other, one *must* be the exact opposite of the other. With the example he gave, it sounded fairly impressive, and it took me a while to be able to explain my disagreement.

Saying, for one claim to contradict another, that one must be the *exact* opposite of the other, its mirror image, is like saying that you can only have an auto collision if the two cars are the same kind of car, with the same shape, and they must be perfectly aligned when they hit each other--because if there's part of one car that doesn't touch the other car, then there hasn't been a *real* collision.

That is simply wrong. In the world of cars, only the tiniest fraction of collisions are two identical cars, hitting each other dead center to dead center. When there's a collision, it is usually two different things which hit off center. And the same is true of ideas. Most collisions in the realm of ideas are two very different things, *not* mirror images. What happens is that one piece of one of them, perhaps the leftmost edge of the bumper, hits one piece of the other, *and in both that one piece is connected to the whole structure*. There is much more involved in the collision, on *both* sides, than that one little bit.

A debate many Christians care about, the debate between the feminist-like egalitarians and the more traditional complementarians, is interesting. (I'll say 'complementarian' for now, even though I don't like the term.) It is interesting as an example of a debate where the collision is *not* between mirror images. Egalitarianism is not the mirror image of complementarianism, and complementarianism is not the mirror image of egalitarianism. They are very different beasts from each other.

Although this is only the outer shell, egalitarians are usually better communicators than complementarians. Most egalitarians make an explicit claim and communicate it very powerfully. Complementarians usually have trouble *explaining* their position, let alone presenting it as compellingly as egalitarians do. This has the effect that people on *both* sides have a much clearer picture of what egalitarian stands for than what complementarianism stands for. The egalitarian claim is often backed by a coherent argument, while the complementarian claim may have Biblical proof texts but often has little else.

I would like to try and suggest what complementarians have so much trouble explaining.

Colors

When I took a cognitive science class, the professor explained a problem for cognitive science: 'qualia'. A computer can represent red and green as two different things. As far as theory problems go, that's *easy* to take care of. The problem is that the computer knows red and green are different only as we can know that two numbers are different. It can't deal with the redness of the red or the greenness of the green: in other words it lacks *qualia*. It can know things are different, but not experience them as really, *quali*tatively different.

Some people can only hear complementarianism as rationalising, "White is brighter than black." Yet it is foundationally a claim of, "Red is red and green is green."

I don't like the term 'complementarian.' It tells part of the truth, but not enough--a property you can see, but not the essence. I would suggest the term 'qualitarian,' for a belief in qualia and qualitative differences. The term's not perfect either, but it's describing some of the substance rather than detail. From here on I'll say 'qualitarian' rather than 'complementarian' to emphasise that there are qualia involved.

With that mentioned, I'd like to make the most unpalatable of my claims next, and hope that if the reader will be generous enough not to write me off yet, I may be able to make some coherent sense.

The Great Chain of Being

This is something that was important to many Christians and which encapsulates a way of looking on the world that *can* be understood, but takes effort.

God

Angels

Humans

Animals

Plants

Rocks

Nothing

The Great Chain of Being was believed for centuries. When the people who believed it were beginning to think like moderns, the Great Chain of Being began to look like the corporate ladder. If there were things above you, you wanted to climb higher because it's not OK to be *you* if someone else is higher than you. If there were things above you, you wanted to look down and sneer because there was something wrong with anything below you. That's how heirarchy looks if the only way you can understand it is as a copy of the corporate ladder.

Before then, people saw it differently. To be somewhere in the middle of the great order was neither a reason to scorn lower things nor covet higher places. Instead, there was a sense of connection. If we are the highest part of the physical creation, then we are to be its custodian and in a real sense its representative. If we are spirits as well, we are not squashed by the fact that God is above us; the one we should worship looks on us in love.

Unlike them, our culture has had centuries of democracy

and waving the banner of equality so high we can forget there are other banners to wave. We strive for equality so hard that it's easy to forget that there can be other kinds of good.

The Great Chain of Being is never explained in the Bible, but it comes out of a certain kind of mindset, a mindset better equipped to deal with certain things.

There's an old joke about two people running from a bear. One stops to put on shoes. The other says, "What are you doing?" The first says, "I'm stopping to put on tennis shoes." The second says, "You can't outrun the bear!" "I don't need to outrun the bear. I only need to outrun you."

One might imagine a medieval speaking with a postmodern. The medieval stands in his niche in the Great Chain of Being and stops. The postmodern says, "Why are you stopping?" The medieval says, "I want to enjoy the glorious place God has granted me in the Great Chain of Being." The postmodern says, "How can you be happy with that? There are others above you." The medieval says, "Not all of life is running from a bear."

What am I trying to say? Am I saying, for instance, that a man is as high above a woman as God is above an angel? *No.* All people--men, women, young, old, infant, red, yellow, black, white--are placed at the same spot on the Great Chain of Being.

The Bible deals with a paradox that may be called "equality with distinction". Paul writes that "In Christ there is no Jew nor Greek", yet claims that the advantage of the Jew is "much in every way." Biblical thinking has room to declare both an equality at deepest level--such as exists between men and women--*and* recognize a distinction. There is no need to culturally argue one away to defend the other. Both are part of the truth. It is good to be part of a Creation that is multilayered, with inequality and not equality between the layers. If this is so, how much more should we be able to consider distinction with fundamental equality without reading the distinction as the corporate ladder's abrasive inequality?

One writer talked about equality in relation to containers being full. To modify her image, Christianity wants *all* of us to be as full as possible. However, it does not want a red paint can to be filled with green paint, nor a green paint can to be filled with red paint. It wants the red and green paint cans to be equally full, but does not conclude that the green can is only full if it has the same volume of red paint as the red paint can. It desires equality in the sense of everyone being full, but does not desire e-*qual*-ity (being without a *qual*-itative difference), in the sense of *qualia* being violated.

Zen and the Art of Un-Framing Questions

May we legitimately project man-like attributes up on to God?

Before answering that question, I'd like to suggest that there are assumptions made by the time that question is asked. The biggest one is that God is gender-neutral, and so any talking about God as masculine is projecting something foreign up on to him.

The qualitarian claim is *not* that we may legitimately project man-like attributes up on to God. It is that God has projected God-like attributes down on to men. Those are different claims.

> A feminist theologian said to a master, "I think it is important that we keep an open mind and avoid confining God to traditional categories of gender."
>
> The master said, "Of course. Why let God reveal himself as masculine when you can confine him to your canons of political correctness?"

I can't shake a vision of an articulate qualitarian giving disturbing answers to someone's questions and sounding like an annoying imitation of a Zen master:

Interlocutor:
What would you say to, "A woman's place is in the

House--and in the Senate!"?

Articulate Qualitarian:
Well, if we're talking about disrespectful, misogysnistic... Wait a minute... Let me respond to the intention *behind* your question.

Do you know the Bible story about the Woman at the Well?

Interlocutor:
Yes! It's one of my favorite stories.

Articulate Qualitarian:
Do you know its cultural context?

Interlocutor:
Not really.

Articulate Qualitarian:
Most Bible stories--including this one--speak for themselves. A few of them are much richer if you know cultural details that make certain things significant.

Every recorded interaction between Jesus and women, Jesus broke rules. To start off, a rabbi wasn't supposed to talk with women. But Jesus *really* broke the rules here.

When a lone woman came out and he asked for water, she was shocked enough to ask *why* he did so. And there's something to her being alone.

Drawing water was a communal women's task. The women of the village would come and draw water *together*; there was a reason why *this* woman was alone: no one would be caught dead with her. Everyone knew that *she* was the village slut.

Her life was dominated by shame. When Jesus said, "...never thirst again," she heard an escape from shamefully drawing water alone, and she asked Jesus to help her hide from it. When he said to call her husband, she gave an evasive and ambiguous reply. He gave a very blunt response: "You are right in saying you have no husband, for you have had five husbands, and the one you have now is not your husband."

Yowch.

Instead of helping her run from her shame, Jesus pulled her *through* it, and she came out the other side, running without any shame, calling, "Come and see a man who told me everything I ever did!"

There's much more, but I want to delve into one specific detail: there was something abnormal about her drawing water alone. Drawing water was women's work. Women's work was backbreaking toil--as was men's work--but it was not done in isolation. It was something done in the company of other people.

It's not just that one culture. There are old European paintings that show a group of women, bent over their washboards, talking and talking. Maybe I'm just romanticizing because I haven't felt how rough washboards are to fingers. But I have a growing doubt that labor-saving devices are all they're cracked up to be. Vacuum cleaners were introduced as a way to lessen the work in the twice-annual task of beating rugs. Somehow each phenomenal new labor-saving technology seems to leave housewives with even more drudgery.

I have sympathy for feminists who say that women are better off doing professional work in community than doing housework in solitary confinement. I think feminists are probably right that the *Leave It to Beaver* arrangement causes women to be lonely and depressed. (I'm not sure that "Turn the clock back, *all* the way back, to *1954!*" represents the best achievement conservatives can claim.)

The traditional arrangement is not Mom, Dad, two kids, and nothing more. Across quite a lot of cultures and quite a lot of history, the usual pattern has kept extended families together (seeing Grandma didn't involve interstate travel), and made those extended families part of an integrated community. From what I've read, women are happier in intentional communities like Reba Place.

Interlocutor:
Do you support the enfranchisement of women?

Articulate Qualitarian:
Let me visit the dict.org website. Webster's 1913 says:

```
Enfranchisement \En*fran"chise*ment\,
      n.
   1. Releasing from slavery or
      custody. --Shak.

   2. Admission to the freedom of a
      corporation or body politic;
      investiture with the privileges
      of free citizens.
```

```
Enfranchisement of copyhold (Eng.
   Law), the conversion of a
   copyhold estate into a
   freehold. --Mozley & W.
```

WordNet seems less helpful; it doesn't really mention the sense you want.

```
enfranchisement
     1: freedom from political
        subjugation or servitude
     2: the act of certifying [syn:
        certification] [ant:
        disenfranchisement]
```

If I were preaching on your question, I might do a Greek-style exegesis and say that your choice of languages fuses the egalitarian request to grant XYZ with the insinuation that their opponents' practice is equivalent to slavery. Wow.

I think you're using loaded language. Would you be willing to restate your question in less loaded terms?

Interlocutor:
Ok, I'll ask a different way, but will you *promise* not to answer with a word-study?

Articulate Qualitarian:
Ok, I won't answer with a word-study unless you ask.

Interlocutor:
Do you believe that women have the *same* long list of rights as men?

Articulate Qualitarian:
Hmm... I'm trying to think about how to answer this

without being misleading...

Interlocutor:
Please answer me *literally.*

Articulate Qualitarian:
I'm afraid I'm going to have to say, "No."

Interlocutor:
But you at least believe that women have *some* rights, correct?

Articulate Qualitarian:
No.

Interlocutor:
What?!?

Articulate Qualitarian:
I said I wouldn't give a word-study...

Is it OK if I give a comparable study of a *concept*?

Interlocutor:
[Quietly counts to ten and takes a deep breath:] Ok.

Articulate Qualitarian:
I don't believe that women have any rights. I don't believe that men have any rights, either. The Bible doesn't use rights like we do. It answers plenty of questions we try to solve with rights: it says we shouldn't murder, steal, and so on. But the older Biblical way of doing this said, "Don't do this," or "Be like Christ," or something like that.

Then this really odd moral framework *based on* rights

came along, and all of a sudden there wasn't a universal law against unjustified killing, but an entitlement not to be killed. At first it seemed not to make much difference. But now more and more of our moral reasoning is in terms of 'rights', which increasingly say, not "Don't do this," or "You must do that," but "Here's the long list of entitlements that the universe *owes* me." And that has meant some truly strange things.

In the context of the concrete issues that qualitarians discuss with egalitarians, the Biblical concept of seeking the good of all is quietly remade into seeking the enfranchisement of all, and so it seems that the big question is whether women get the same rights as men--quite apart from the kind of situation where language comparing your opponents' behavior to slavery is considered polite.

Interlocutor:
Couldn't we listen to, say, Eastern Philosophy?

Articulate Qualitarian:
There's a lot of interesting stuff in Eastern philosophy. The contrast between Confucian and Taoist concepts of virtue, for instance, is interesting and worth exploring, especially in *this* nexus. I'm really drawing a blank as to how one could get a rights-based framework from Asian philosophy. And I'm not sure African mindsets would be much more of a help, for instance. Even if you read one Kwaanza pamphlet, it's hard to see how individual rights could come from the seven African values. The value of Ujima, or collective work and responsibility, speaks even less of individual rights than, "Ask not what your country can do for you, but what you can do for your country."

Interlocutor:
Ok, let me change the subject slightly. Would you acknowledge that Paul was a progressive?

Articulate Qualitarian:
Hmm... reminds me of a C.S. Lewis book in which Lewis quotes a medieval author. The author is talking about some important Greek philosopher and says, "Now when we come to a difficulty or ambiguity, we should always ascribe the views most worthy of a man of his stature."

Lewis's big complaint was that this kind of respect *always* reads into an author the biases and assumptions of the reader's age. It honors the author enough to think he believed what we call important, but not enough that the author can disagree with our assumptions *and be able to correct us*.

When we ask if Paul is a progressive, there are two basic options. Either we say that Paul was not a progressive, and relegate him to our understanding of a misogynist, or we generously overlook a passage here and there and generously include him as one of our progressives.

It seems that *neither* response allows Paul to be an authority who knows something we don't.

On second thought, maybe it's a *good* thing there aren't too many articulate qualitarians.

Men are from Mars, Women are from Venus... and Gender Psychologists are from the Moon

When pop psychology talks about gender, it is trying to make academic knowledge available to the rest of us. An academic textbook by Em Griffin illustrates Deborah Tannen's theories, saying, "Jan hopes she's marrying a 'big ear'." This thread is picked up very well in popular works.

William Harley's *His Needs, Her Needs* is a sort of Christianized *Men are from Mars, Women are from Venus*. Harley devotes a full chapter to explaining that one of the most foundational needs for a husband to understand is a woman's need for listening. He devotes a full chapter to convincing husbands that it is essential that they listen to everything their wives want to say. It was perhaps because reading this work (and *Men are From Mars, Women are From Venus*, part of *You Just Don't Understand*, etc.) that I was shocked when I reread C.S. Lewis's *That Hideous Strength*. It was much more than Mother Dimble's words, "Husbands were made to be talked to. It helps them concentrate their minds on what they're reading..."

The shock was deep. It wasn't like having a rug pulled out from under your feet. It was more like standing with your feet on bare floor and having the *floor* pulled out from under your feet.

The gender books I'd read, both Christian and non-Christian, made a seamless fusion of the basic raw material, and one *particular* interpretation. The interpretation was as hard to doubt as the raw material itself--and one couldn't really see the fusion as something that *can* be questioned. It was like looking at a number of startlingly accurate pictures of scenes on earth--and then realising that all the pictures were taken from the moon.

That Hideous Strength suggests an answer to the question, "How else could it be?" I'm hesitant to suggest everyone else will have the same experience, but...

If we look at a Hollywood movie targeting young men,

there will be violent action, a fast pace, and a sense of adventure. A movie made for young women will have people talking and delving into emotions as they grow closer, as they grow into more mature relationships. If we sum these up in a single word, the men's movie is full of *action*, and the women's movie is filled with *relationship*.

Aristotle characterized masculinity as active and femininity as passive. It seems clear to me that he was grappling with a real thing, the same thing that shapes our movie offerings. It also seems clear that he didn't quite get it right. Masculinity is active. That much is correct. But femininity is not described by the *absence* of such action. It's described by the *presence* of relationship. It seems that the following can be said:

- Aristotle was grappling with, and trying to understand, something real.
- Even though he's observing something real, his interpretation was skewed.

These two things didn't stop with Aristotle. If a thinker as brilliant as Aristotle fell into this trap, maybe gender psychology is also liable to stumble this way, too. (Or at least *today's* gender psychology stumbles this way. If you're willing to listen to people who look and talk a bit different and are a bit older than us, Charles Shedd's *Letters to Karen* and *Letters to Philip* are examples of slightly older books worth the time to look at.)

Christian Teaching

About this point, I expect a question like, "Ok, men reflect the masculine side of God. But don't you have a place for femininity, and can't women reflect the feminine side of God?"

This is a serious question, and it reflects a serious concern. Many Hindus believe that everything is either part of God or evil: your inmost spirit is a real part of God, and your body is intrinsically evil and illusory like everything else physical. I'm told that Genesis 1 was quite a shocker when it appeared--not, so much, because it says we're made in the image of God, but because after the stars, rocks, plants, and animals were created, the text keeps on saying, "And God saw that it was *good*." That's really a staggering suggestion, if you knew the other nations' creation stories. The Babylonians believed that the god Marduk killed the demoness Tiamat, tore her dragon carcass apart, and made half of it the land and half of it the sky. So your body and mine, every forest, every star, is part of a demon's carcass that happens to be left over after a battle.

Please think about this claim for a minute, and then look at part of Genesis 1:

- Creation didn't happen as a secondary result of divine combat. God created the world because he specifically wanted to do so.
- Physical matter, and life, and everything else, is *good.*
- God made us in his image. Only then was his creation very good, and complete.

One thing that comes out of these things is that *God can create good.* God created the physical world without being physical. Our bodies, indeed the whole natural world, are good, because God created something outside of himself. Femininity is like this, only much more so. *Femininity is a created good,* and it is much more beautiful, more mysterious, more wondrous, more powerful thing than physical matter. People are the unique creation where matter meets spirit--no other creation can claim that. Women are the unique point where spirit meets the very apex of femininity.

Every woman is a mystery, and every man is a king. To be a Christian man is to be made like the King of Kings and Lord of Lords. There is something kingly and lordly about manhood. Part of this is understood when you realize that this does *not* mean domineering other people and standing above them, but standing under them, like the servant king who washed feet. The sign and sigil of male authority is not a crown of gold, but a crown of thorns.

But all this is a hint. I give sketch here and there, and I hope less to provide an inescapable logical framework than suggest entry points that can look into the Bible and see these things.

I'd like to give a glimpse of the qualities:

Qualia

Lord Adam, Dragonslayer

If you could see Adam, you would see a knight, in burnished armor brightly gleaming, astride a white horse. What you wouldn't see is why the armor shines brightly. It is not burnished by him, nor any other human hands, but the claws of the dragons he wars against. Under his helmet is a lion's mane of thick hair and beard. Under his breastplate are scars, some quite close to his heart.

This knight errant yearns for quests. Something difficult, something dangerous, something active. Some place to prove himself by serving in a costly way. He longs for that battle when his blood will mingle with that of his fellow warriors and he may at last embark on the last great adventure.

He has a lord above him, to whom he owes allegiance and honor. He is also a mentor, turning his face to a squires whom he focuses on and draws up. He draws them, as he was drawn, out of the comfort of home, into the mysteries of life, and into the company of men and society to reconnect more deeply. He has tried to explain that siring a child is something an impudent youth can do, but being a spiritual father is the mark of a *man*.

Once his mind is on a task, it moves forward from beginning to end. It moves with the force of an avalanche. He does one task at a time, and wants to do it well.

There is another side to his seriousness. He can be deadly serious, but there is a merry twinkle in his eye. His force and his energy are too much to contain, and he is capable of catching people off guard. (Especially in his practical jokes.) Like the lion, he is not safe and not tame; he is both serious and silly, and can astound in both. When he plays with children, playing with him is both like playing with a kitten and playing with a thunderstorm.

To his lady Adam turns with reverence. She is a wonder to him. The extravagance of the quests she bids him and he embarks on, is a spectacular offshoot of his more quiet service in private. Though Adam would never see it this way, he is taller when he bows and kisses her hand, and richer when he gives her a costly gift.

His honor is his life, and wants to live and act as a son of God. He believes that faith *works*, and strives to show virtue and behave in a manner worthy of Christ.

Favorite Scripture Passage:

"And being found in human form he humbled himself and became obedient unto death, even death on a cross. Therefore God has highly exalted him and bestowed on him the name which is above every name, that at the name of Jesus every knee should bow, in heaven and on earth and under the earth, and every tongue confess that Jesus Christ is Lord, to the glory of God the Father."

A Quote:

"God, give me mountains to climb and the strength for climbing."

Lady Eve, Poet's Heart

If you could see Eve at her best, she would be beside a fire, inside a great hall. She would be stoking a fire with one hand, another hand would call forth forth music from a silver harp, another hand would be writing a letter, and she would use both hands to embrace the sorrowing child on her lap in comforting love. And she would do this lightly, joyfully, with a smile from the other side of pain. Though Eve sits still, one can almost see her dancing. It would take time to see all her many layers of beauty... if that were even possible. *What is the secret behind her enigmatic smile? What deep mysteries lie hidden in her heart of hearts?*

Her beauty is as a rose: a ladder of thorns leads up to a flower so exquisite as to be called God's autograph. She toils hard, and it is difficult to see lines of pain in her face only because she has worked through them so that they have become part of her joy. She knows a mother's worry, and she looks on others with a mother's caring eyes. She looks with the joy on the other side of sorrow.

Her home is her castle, and it is a castle she tries to run well. She runs the castle in an orderly and efficient manner, and as the lady in charge, she handles well a great many things that her lord wouldn't know how to begin doing. The castle is their castle, of course, but there are things that need attending to so that Adam can continue slaying dragons. Yet to say that is to put last things first. The reason she handles so many taxing details is that Adam is the light of her life, her king and her lord, her bright morning star.

She turns to her loom as a place to make wall hangings. At least, that's what someone would say if he missed the point completely. She makes beautiful wall hangings, but there's more.

The loom is a centering place for her, a quieting place. After other things happen that take processing, she settles into that peace. Her heart is quieted as she lets it all sort out.

That quieting is not far from her mystic's heart. She is mystery and lives in connection with the mystery of faith. There is One she is closer to than her lord, and presence, mystical communion, dwelling in the presence of the divine, is precious to her.

Favorite Scripture Passage:

"Why do you trouble the woman? For she has done a beautiful thing to me. For you always have the poor with you, but you will not always have me. In pouring this ointment on my body she has done it to prepare me for burial. Truly, I say to you, wherever this gospel is preached in the whole world, what she has done will be told in memory of her."

A Quote:

"Little surprises and big hugs and kisses.
Musical dances and bright reminisces,
Quiet with stories and roast leg of lamb,
People who value me for who I am,
Something to say and someone who will hear it,
A home in good order and a mystical spirit,
Warm fireside chats and a minstrel who sings,
These are a few of my favorite things."

With thanks to Martin, Phil, Mary, Xenia, Patrick, Yoby, Mom, and Kathryn.

What the Present Debate Won't Tell You about Headship

I am writing about head and body (headship). And I say "headship" with hesitation, because in today's world asserting "headship" means, "defending traditional gender roles against feminism." And that maybe important, but I want to talk about something larger, something that will be missed if "headship" means nothing more than "one position in the feminist controversy."

One speaker didn't like people entering Church and saying, "It's so good to enter the Lord's presence." He said, "Where were you all week? How did you escape the Lord's presence?" And whatever Church is, it is absolutely not entering the one place where God is present. At least, it's not stepping out of some imaginary place where God simply can't be found.

But if we are always in the Lord's presence, that doesn't mean that Church isn't special. It is special, and it is the head of living in God's presence for all of our lives. Our time in Church is an example of headship. Worshipping God in Church is the head of a life of worship, and it is the head of a body.

There is something special about our time in Church. But the way we live our lives, our "body" of time spent, manifests that glory in a different way. Christ didn't say that people will know we are his disciples by our "official" worship, however much God's blessing may rest on it. Christ said instead that all people will know we are his disciples by this, that we love one another. That isn't primarily in Church. That's in our day to day lives. If our time in Church crystallizes a life of worship, our love for one another is to manifest it. And that is the place of the body.

The relationship between head and body is the relationship between corporate worship and our lives as a whole. The body manifests the glory of the head. In my head I can decide to walk to a friend's house. But the head needs the body and the body needs the head, and I can only go to a friend's house if my head's decision to visit a friend's house is lived out in my body. "The head cannot say to the feet, 'I have no need of you.'"

The Father is the head of the Son. "No man can see God and live." God the Father is utterly beyond us; he transcends anything we could know; he is pure glory. If we were to have direct contact with him, we would be destroyed. And yet the Son is equal to the Father; the Son is just as far beyond this Creation, but there is a difference. The Son is the bridge between God and man, and God and his Creation. God the Father created the world through the Son, and the Son is just as glorious as the Father, but the Son can touch us without destroying us. The Father displays himself through the Son. The Father's love came to earth through the Son. The Father's wish that we may be made divine is possible precisely because the Son became man. And finally we can know the Father through the Son. If you have seen the Son, you have seen the Father.

We read in the New Testament that Christ is the head of man, that Christ is the head of all authority, that Christ is the head of the Church, and that Christ is the head of the whole Creation. If we think, with people today, that to have any authority over us, any head, is degrading, then we have to resent a lot more than a husband's headship to his wife. But that's not the only option. When Christ is the head of the cosmos, there is more than authority going on, even if we have a negative view of authority. Our Orthodox understanding that the Son of God became a man that men might become the sons of God, that the divine became human that the human might become divine, expresses what the headship of Christ means. Christ is the head, and that means that the Church is drawn up in his divinity. If we are the body of Christ the head, that doesn't mean we're just under his authority. It means that we are a part of him and share in his divinity. The teaching that we share in his divinity is very tightly connected to the teaching of "recapitulation", or "re-heading," where Christ being the head of the Church, and our sharing in Christ's divinity, are two sides of the same coin. Christ is the head, and we, the body, make Christ manifest to the world. Some people may not know Christ except what they see in us. We cannot have Christ as our head without being a manifestation of his glory, and if Christ is the head of the Creation and Christ is the head of the Church, that means that when we worship, inside this building and in our daily lives, we are leading the whole visible Creation in turning to God in glory, and living the life of Heaven here on earth.

Christ is the head of the whole Creation, not just the Church. Christ isn't just concerned with his people, but the whole created world. By him and through him all things were created. Icons, which reflect the full implications Christ's headship over his Creation, exist precisely because Christ is the head of the whole Creation. We use a censer, a building, icons, water, flowers, and other aspects of our matter-embracing religion as representatives of the whole material Creation over which Christ is head. Christ doesn't tell us to be spiritual as spirits who are unfortunately trapped in matter; far from it, we are the crowning jewel of the material Creation, and Christ's headship glorifies the whole Creation and makes it foundational to how we are saved. The universe is a symbol that manifests the glory of its head, Christ.

One example of headship that is immediate to me, although I don't know how immediate it is to the rest of you, is artistic creation. I create, write, and program, and in a very real sense I am at my fullest when I create. When I create, at first there is a hazy idea that I don't understand very well. Then I listen to it, and begin struggling with it, trying to understand my creation, and even if I am wrestling with it, I am wrestling less to dominate it than to get myself out of its way so I can help bring it into being. If in one sense I wrestle with it, in another sense I am wrestling with myself to let my creation be what it should be. If I were to simply dominate my creation, I would crush it, breaking its spirit. My best creations are those which I serve, where I use my headship to give my creations freedom and cooperate with them so that they are greater than if I did not give my creations room to breathe. My best work comes, not when I decide, "I am going to create," but when I cooperate with a creation, love it, serve it, and help it to become real, the creation becomes a share of my spirit.

A great many writers could say that, and I don't think this is something that is only found in writing, but how something far more general plays out. All of us are called to exercise headship over our work. In a family, the father is the head of the household and the mother is the heart of the household. The mother's headship over work in the home provides ten thousand touches that make a house a home. A mother's headship over the home is as much human headship over one's work as my headship over my creations and writing. What I do when I create is love my creation, serve it, develop it, work with God and with my creation to help it be real. If I'm not mistaken, when a woman makes a house into a real home, she loves it, serves it, develops it, and works with God and what she has to make it real. When a woman makes a house into a warm and inviting home, *that's headship.*

What is the relationship between women and the home? In societies where people have best been able to honor what the Bible says about men's and women's roles, there is a strong association between women and the home. The home, in those societies, was the main focus of business, charity work, and education, besides the much narrower role played by a home today. To say that women were mainly in the home is to say that they held an important place in one of society's important institutions, an institution that was the chief home of business, education, hospitality, and what would today be insurance, and held many responsibilities that are denied to housewives today. The isolation felt by many housewives today was much less an issue because women worked together with other women; like men, they worked in adult company. I believe there should be an association between women and the home, and I believe the home should be respected and influential. And, for that matter, I believe that both men and women are sold short with the options they have today. But instead of going too deep into that sort of question, important as it may be, I would like to look at what headship means.

The sanctuary is the head of the nave. Part of what that means is that there is something richer than either if there were just an sanctuary or just a nave. But we'll miss something fundamental if we only say that the sanctuary is more glorious to the nave. They are connected and part of the same body. They are part of the same organism, and the sanctuary manifests the glory of the sanctuary. There is also a head-body relation between the saint and the icon. Or between the reality a symbol represents, and a symbol. Or between Heaven and earth. Bringing Heaven down to earth is a right ordering of this world. Heaven isn't just something that happens after death after we serve God by suffering in this world. "Eye has not seen, ear has not heard, nor has any heart imagined what God has prepared for those who love him," but God wants to work Heaven in our lives, beginning here and now. If we are bringing Heaven down to earth, we are realizing God's design that Heaven be the head of earth, in the fullness of what headship means.

What about husbands and wives? There's something that we'll miss today if we just expect wives to submit to their husbands, even if we recognized that that's tied to an even more difficult assignment for husbands, loving their wives on the model of Christ giving up his own life for the Church. And we need to be countercultural, but there's something we'll miss if we just react to the currents in society that make this unattractive. Quite a few heresies got their start in reactions against older heresies; it is spiritually dangerous to simply react against errors, and if feminism might have problems, simply reacting to feminism is likely to have problems. Wives should submit to their husbands, and husbands should love their wives with a costly love, but there's more.

It bothers me when conservatives say, "I want to turn the clock back... all the way back... *to 1954*!" If we're just reacting against some feminists when they say women should be strong and independent, and have no further reference point, we're likely to defend a femininity that says that women are weak and passive. What's wrong with that? For starters, it's not Biblical.

If you want to know God's version of femininity, read the conclusion of Proverbs. The opening of this conclusion is often translated, "Who can find a good wife?" That's too weak. It is better translated as, "Who can find a wife of **valor**," with "valor" being a word that could be used of a mighty soldier. She is strong--*physically* strong. The text explicitly mentions her powerful arms. She is active in commerce and charity. There are important differences between this and the feminist picture, but if we are defending an un-Biblical ideal for womanhood, some delicate thing that can't do anything and is always in a swoon, then our reaction against feminism isn't going to put us in a much better spot.

And men should be men, but that doesn't mean that men should be rugged individuals who say, "I am the master of my fate: I am the captain of my soul!" That is as wrong as saying that Biblical femininity is weak and passive. Perhaps men should be rugged, but to be a man is to be under authority. Trying to be the captain of your soul is spiritually toxic, and perhaps blasphemous. There is one person who can say, "I am the captain of my soul," and it isn't Christ. Not even Christ can say that, but only God the Father. Christ's glory was to be the Son of God, so that the Father was the captain of his soul, and he did the Father's work. Even Christ was under the headship of the Father, and if you read what John says about the Father and the Son, the fact that Christ was under headship, under authority, is part of his dignity and his own authority. To be a man is, if things are going well, to be a contributing member of a community, and in submission to its authority. Individualism is a severe distortion of masculinity; it may not be feminine, but it is hardly characteristic of healthy masculinity. There are a lot of false and destructive pictures of what a man should be, as well as what a woman should be.

If simply reacting against feminism is a way to miss what it means to be a man and what it means to be a woman, it is also a way to miss something more, to miss a broader glory. This something more is foundational to the structure of reality; it is a resonance not only with God's Creation, but within the nature of God and how the Father's glory is shown through the Son. This something more is in continuity with God's headship to Christ, Christ's headship to the Church, Christ's headship to the cosmos, Heaven's headship to earth, the sanctuary's headship to the nave, the spiritual world's headship to the physical world, the soul's headship to the body, contemplation's headship to action, and other manifestations of a headship relation. On the Sunday of Orthodoxy, we proclaim:

> ...Thus we declare, thus we assert, thus we preach Christ our true God, and honor as Saints in words, in writings, in thoughts, in sacrifices, in churches, in Holy Icons; on the one hand worshipping and reverencing Christ as God and Lord, and on the other hand honoring as true servants of the same Lord of all and accordingly offering them veneration... This is the Faith of the Apostles, this is the Faith of the Fathers, this is the Faith of the Orthodox, this is the Faith which has established the Universe.

What does this have to do with heads and bodies? The word "icon" itself means a body, and its role is to manifest the glory of the saints, as the saints are to manifest the glory of God.

We don't have a choice about whether we will live in a universe with headship, but we do have a choice whether to work with the grain or against it, work with it to our profit or fight it to our detriment. Let's make headship part of how we rejoice in God and his Creation.

A Strange Picture

As I walked through the gallery, I immediately stopped when I saw one painting. As I stopped and looked at it, I became more and more deeply puzzled. I'm not sure how to describe the picture.

It was a picture of a city, viewed from a high vantage point. It was a very beautiful city, with houses and towers and streets and parks. As I stood there, I thought for a moment that I heard the sound of children playing--and I looked, but I was the only one present.

This made all the more puzzling the fact that it was a disturbing picture--chilling even. It was not disturbing in the sense that a picture of the Crucifixion is disturbing, where the very beauty is what makes it disturbing. I tried to see what part might be causing it, and met frustration. It seemed that the beauty was itself what was wrong--but that couldn't be right, because when I looked more closely I saw that the city was even more beautiful than I had imagined. The best way I could explain it to myself was that the ugliness of the picture could not exist except for an inestimable beauty. It was like an unflattering picture of an attractive friend--you can see your friend's good looks, but the picture shows your friend in an ugly way. You have to fight the picture to really see your friend's beauty--and I realized that I was fighting the picture to see the city's real beauty. It was a shallow picture of something profound, and it was perverse. An artist who paints a picture helps you to see through his eyes--most help you to see a beauty that you could not see if you were standing in the same spot and looking. This was like looking at a mountaintop through a pair of eyes that were blind, with a blindness far more terrible, far more crippling, than any blindness that is merely physical. I stepped back in nausea.

I leaned against a pillar for support, and my eyes fell to the bottom of the frame. I glanced on the picture's title: *Pornography.*

The Patriarchy We Object To

Tell me what kind of patriarchy you object to. As Orthodox, we probably object to that kind of patriarchy as well.

There was one chaplain at a university who, whenever a student would come in and say, "I don't believe in God," would answer, "Tell me what kind of God you don't believe in. I probably don't believe in that kind of God either." And he really had something in common with them. He didn't believe in a God who was a vindictive judge, or a God who was responsible for all the evil in this world, or a God who was arbitrary and damned people for never hearing of him. And the chaplain wasn't just making a rhetorical exercise; he didn't believe in many kinds of "God" any more than the students who were kind enough to come and tell him they didn't believe in God. He really had something in common with them.

There was one book I was reading which was trying to recover women's wisdom from patriarchy. I was amazed when I was reading it, as it talked about the holistic, united character of women's knowing, and how women's knowledge is relational, how women know by participating. What amazed me was how much it had in common with Orthodox description of knowledge, because the Orthodox understanding of knowledge is based off an essential unity and knows by relating, participating, drinking, rather than by analyzing and taking apart and knowing things by keeping track of a systematic map.

What Orthodoxy in the West would seek to recover from the West looks a lot like what feminism would like to recover from patriarchy. Part of what may confuse the issue is that feminism lumps together two very different forces as "patriarchy." One of these forces is classical tradition, and the other is something funny that's been going on for several hundred years in which certain men have defaced society by despising it and trying to make it manly.

The reason that women's holistic, connected knowledge is countercultural is something we'll miss if we only use the category of "patriarchy". The educational system, for instance, makes very little use of this knowledge, not because patriarchy has always devalued women's ways of knowing, but something very different. The reason that there's something countercultural to women's holistic, connected knowledge is that that is a basic human way of knowing, and men can be separated from it more easily than women, but it's a distortion of manhood to marginalize that way of knowing. And there has been a massive effort, macho in the worst way, that despised how society used to work, assumed that something is traditional it must be the women's despicable way of doing things, and taken one feature of masculine knowledge and used it to uproot the the places for other ways of knowing that are important to both *men* and women. There are two quite different forces lumped together in the category of "patriarchy." One is the tradition proper, and the other is "masculism" (or at least I call it that), and what feminism sees as patriarchy is what's left over of the tradition after masculism has defaced it by trying to make it "masculine," on the assumption that if something was in the tradition, that was all you needed to know, in order to attack it as being unfit for men. *"Masculism" is what happens when you cross immature masculinity with the effort to destroy whatever you need to make room for your version of Utopia.* What is left of the tradition today, and what feminism knows as "patriarchy," is a bit like what's left of a house after it's been burned down.

With apologies to G.K. Chesterton, the Orthodox and feminists only ask to get their heads into the Heavens. It is the masculists who try to fit the Heavens into their heads, and it is their heads that split. This basic difference between knowing as exaltation and expansion, participating in something and allowing one's head to be raised in the Heavens, and domination and mastery that compresses the Heavens so they will fit in one's head, is the difference between what "knowing" means to both feminists and Orthodox, and what it means to masculists.

The difference between Orthodoxy and feminism is this. Orthodoxy has to a very large measure preserved the tradition. When it objects to masculism, it is objecting to an intrusion that affects something it is keeping. It is a guard trying to protect a treasure. Where Orthodoxy is a guard trying to protect a treasure, feminism is a treasure hunter trying to find something that world has lost. It is a scout rather than a guard. (And yes, I'm pulling images from my masculine mind.) Feminism is shaped by masculism, and I'd like to clarify what I mean by this. I don't mean in *any* sense that feminism wants to serve as a rubber stamp committee for masculism. The feminist struggle is largely a struggle to address the problems created by masculism. that's pretty foundational. But people that rebel against something tend to keep a lot of that something's assumptions, and feminism is a lot like masculism because in a culture as deeply affected by masculism as much of the West, masculism is the air people breathe. (People can't stop breathing their air, whatever culture they're in.) For one example of this, masculism assumed that anything in the tradition was womanish and therefore unfit for men, and feminism inherited a basic approach from masculism when it assumed that anything in tradition was patriarchal and therefore unfit for women. It's a masculist rather than traditional way of approaching society. Orthodoxy has been affected by masculism to some degree, but it's trying to preserve the Orthodox faith, where feminism has been shaped by masculism to a much greater degree and is trying to rebel against the air its members breathe. Feminism is a progressive series of attempts to reform masculism for women; if you look at its first form, it said, "Women should be treated better. They should be treated like men." Later forms of feminism have seen that there are problems with that approach, but they have been reacting to a composite of masculism and earlier versions of feminism. Feminism has been a scout, rather than a guard.

I say that feminism has been a scout rather than a guard, not to criticize, but to suggest that Orthodoxy has been given something that feminism reaches for, but does not have in full. It is a bit like the difference between maintaining a car and trying to go through a junkyard with the wrecks of many magnificent things and reconstruct a working vehicle. In a junkyard, one sees the imprint of many things; one sees the twisted remains of quite a few items that would be good to have. And one can probably assemble things, get some measure of functionality, perhaps hobble together a working bicycle. And if one does not have a working car, there is something very impressive about doing one's best to assemble something workable from the wreckage. It is perhaps not the best manners to criticize someone who has combined parts to make a genuinely working bicycle and say, "But you were not given a working car!"

But in Orthodoxy, there is a very different use of time. Orthodox do not simply spend time filling the gas tank (there are many necessities in faith like filling a gas tank) and maintaining the car (which we periodically break), necessary as those may be. Having a car is primarily about living life as it is lived when you can drive. It is about being able to travel and visit people. It is about having more jobs open to you. If a car isn't working, dealing with the car means trying to do whatever you can to get it working. It means thinking about how to fix it. And feminism is trying to correct masculism. If a car *is* working, dealing with the car is about what it can let you do. It's like how when you're sick, your mind is on getting well and on your health. If you're healthy, you don't think about your health unless you choose to. You're free to *enjoy* your health by focusing on non-health-related pursuits.

What does Orthodoxy have to contribute to feminism? To begin with, it's not simply a project by men. Feminist tends to assume that whatever is in patriarchy is there because all-powerful men have imposed it on women, or to put things in unflattering terms women have contributed little of substance to patriarchal society. That may have truth as regards masculism, but Orthodoxy is the property of both men and women (and boys and girls), and it is a gross mischaracterization to only look at the people who hold positions of power.

Feminists have made bitter criticism of Prozac being used to mask the depression caused by many housewives' loneliness and isolation. Housewives who do not work outside the home have much more than housework to deal with; they have loneliness and isolation from adult company. And perhaps, feminists may icily say, if a woman under those conditions is depressed, this does not necessarily mean Prozac is appropriate. Maybe, just maybe, the icy voice tells us, the solution is to change those conditions instead of misusing antidepressants to mask the quite *natural* depression those conditions create. Feminists are offended that women are confined to a place outside of society's real life and doing housework in solitary confinement. One of the most offensive things you can say, if there is no irony or humor in your voice, is, "*A woman's place is in the house!*" (and not add, "and in the Senate!")

But Orthodoxy looks at it differently, or at least Orthodox culture tends to work out differently. And, like many alien cultures, things have a very different meaning. The home has a different meaning. When people say "family" today, we think of a nuclear family. Then it was extended family, and thinking of an extended family without a nuclear family would have been as odd to people then as it would be odd today to take your favorite food and then be completely unable to eat anything else. Traditional society, *real* traditional society, did not ask women to work in isolation. Both men and women worked in adult company. And the home itself... In traditional society, the home was the primary place where economic activity occurred. In traditional society, the home was the primary place where charitable work occurred. In traditional society, the home took care of what we would now call insurance. In traditional society, the home was the primary place where education occured. Masculism has stripped away layer after layer of what the home was. In Orthodox culture, in truly Orthodox culture that has treasures that have been dismantled in the West, a woman's place really *is* in the home, but it means something totally different from what a feminist cringes at in the words, "A woman's place is in the house!"

America has largely failed to distinguish between what feminism says and women's interests, so people think that if you are for women, you must agree with feminism. Saying "I oppose feminism because I am for women's interests" seems not only false but a contradiction in terms, like saying "I'm expanding the text of this webpage so it will be more concise." It's not like more thoughtful Catholics today, who say, "I have thought, and I understand why many people distinguish or even oppose the teachings of the Catholic Church with God's truth. But my considered judgment is that God reveals his truth through the living magisterium of the Catholic Church." It's more like what the Reformers faced, where people could not see what on earth you meant if you said that God's truth and the Catholic Church's teaching were not automatically the same thing.

In this culture, someone who is trying to be pro-woman will ordinarily reach for feminism as the proper vehicle, just as someone who wants to understand the natural world will reach for science as the proper vehicle for that desire; "understanding the human body" is invariably read as "learning scientific theories about the body's work," and not "take a massage/dance/martial arts class", or "learn what religions and cultures have seen in the meaning of the human body." A great many societies pursued a deep understanding of the human body without expressing that desire the way Western science pursues it. They taught people to come to a better knowledge **of** their bodies--and I mean "of," not just "about"--the kind of relational, drinking knowledge that feminists and Orthodox value, and not just a list of abstract propositions from dissecting a cadaver (a practice which some cultures regard as "impious and disgusting"--C.S. Lewis). They taught people to develop, nurture, and discipline their bodies so that there was a right relationship between body and spirit. They taught people to see the body as belonging a world of meaning, symbol, and spiritual depth--cultures where "How does it work?" takes a back seat to a deeper question: "Why? What does it mean?" Orthodoxy at its best still *does* teach these things. But Western culture has absorbed the scientific spirit that most people genuinely cannot see what "understanding the body" could mean besides "learning scientific theories about the body." And, in this context, it seems like a deceitful sleight of hand when someone says, "I want to help you understand the body" and then offers help in ways of moving one's body.

But I want to talk about some things that are missed within this set of assumptions. Feminism *can* speak for women's interests. It normally claims to. And women are ill-served by an arrangement when people assume that criticism of feminism is at the expense of women's interests. We need to open a door that American culture does not open. We need to open the possibility of being willing to challenge feminism in order to further women's interests. Not on all points, but if we never open that door, disturbing things can happen.

If you ask someone outside of feminism who "the enemy" is to feminists, the common misunderstanding is, "Nonfeminist men." And that's certainly part of the problem and not part of the solution, but the real vitriol feeds into jokes like "How many men does it take to open a beer?--She should have it open when she brings it to him." The real vitriol is reserved for the contented housewife who wants to be married, have children, and make a home, and not have a professional career because of what she values in homemaking itself.

Feminism is against "patriarchy." That means that much that is positive in the tradition is attacked along with masculism. That means that whatever the tradition provided for women is interpreted as harmful to women, even if it benefits women.

Wendy Shalit makes an interesting argument in A Return to Modesty that sexual modesty is not something men have imposed on women against their nature for men's benefit; it is first and foremost a womanly virtue that protects women. We now have a defaced version of traditional society, but to start by assuming that almost everything in the culture is a patriarchal imposition that benefits only men, sets the stage for throwing out a great many things that are important for women. It sets the stage, in fact, for completing the attack that masculism began. (The effect of throwing out things that strike you as patriarchal on a culture has much the same effect as killing off species in an ecosystem because you find them unpleasant. It is an interconnected, interdependent, and organic whole that all its members need. That's not quite the right way of saying it, but this image has a grain of truth.) Masculism scorned the traditional place for men, and was masculine only in that it rebelled against perceivedly feminine virtue. Feminism does not include a large number of women's voices in America and an even larger number worldwide--because feminism lumps them all together in "The Enemy." At times feminism can look anti-woman.

So everything will be OK if we resist feminism? No. First, if the tradition is right--let us say, in the controversial point that associates women with the home--that doesn't make much sense of today's options that don't really let women be women and don't let men be men. What is the closest equivalent to women reigning in one of society's most important institions? Is it to be a housewife with a lunchtime discussion group, which seems to work wonders for depression caused by loneliness? Is it for women to keep house and work part time? Is it to work full time, and find an appropriate division of labor with their husbands? I have trouble telling which of these is best, and it doesn't help matters to choose an option just because it bothers feminists. I think that women (and, for that matter, men) have an impoverished set of options today. Unfortunately, some of the most practical questions are also the ones that are hardest to answer.

Second and more importantly, reacting against feminism, or much of anything else, is intrinsically dangerous. If feminism has problems, we would be well advised to remember that heresies often start when people react against other heresies and say that the truth is so important they should resist that heresy as much as they can. Reactions against heresy are often heresy.

Let me explain how not to respond to feminism's picture of what men should be. You could say that feminism wants women to be more like men and men to be more like women, and that has a significant amount of truth. But if you dig in and say that men should be rugged and independent and say, "I am the master of my fate. I am the captain of my soul!", and women should be weak, passive creatures that are always in a swoon, there are several major problems.

The phrase "I am the master of my fate. I am the captain of my soul!" is something that nobody but God should say. Someone greater than us is the master of our fate, and someone greater than us is the master of our soul, and that is our glory. To be a man is to be under authority. Perhaps it irks feminists that the Bible tells wives to submit to their husbands as well as telling husbands to love their wives with the greatest and most costly love. (I've heard some first class citizens pointing out that the Bible requires something much heftier of husbands than mere submission--loving *and loving* their wives on the model of Christ going so far as to give up his life for the Church.) But the tradition *absolutely does not* say "Women are to be second-class citizens because they are under men's authority and men are to be first-class citizens because they have the really good position of being free from authority." To be a man is to be under authority, to be a woman is to be under authority, and to be human is to be under authority. To masculism this looks demeaning because immature masculinity resists being under authority or being in community or any other thing that men embrace when they grow up. But Orthodoxy is a call to grow up, and it is a call to men to be contributing members of a community and to be under authority. To tell men, "Be independent!" is to tell them, "Refuse to grow up!"

What about women? Shouldn't they be passive and dependent? Let's look at one of the Bible's most complete treatments of what a woman should be like. I'll give my own slightly free translation from the Greek version of Proverbs (31:10-31):

> Who can find a valorous wife?
> She is more precious than precious stones.
> Her husband wholeheartedly trusts her, and will have no lack of treasures.
> Her whole life works good for her husband.
> She gathers wool and linen and weaves with her hands.
> She has become like a trading ship from afar, and she gathers her living.
> She rises at night, and gives food to her house, and assigns work to her maids.
> She examines and buys a farm, and plants a vineyard with the fruit of her hands.
> She girds her loins with strength and strengthens her arms for work.
> She tastes how good it is to work, and her candle stays lit the whole night long.
> She reaches her hands to collective work, and applies her hands to the spindle.
> She opens her hands to the needy, and extends fruit to the poor.
> Her husband does not worry about the men at home when he spends time abroad;
> All her household has clothing.
> She makes double weight clothing for her husband,
> And linen and scarlet for herself.
> Her husband is respected when he engages in important business at the City Hall.
> When he is seated in council with the elders of the land.
> She makes fine linens and sells belts to the Canaanites.
> She opens her mouth with heedfulness and order, and is in

control of her tongue.
She clothes herself in strength and honor, and rejoices in the future.
The ways of her household are secure, and she does not eat the bread of idleness.
She opens her mouth with wisdom, according to the deep law.
Her mercy for her children prepares them, and they grow rich, and her husband praises her.
Many daughters have obtained wealth, and many have worked valiantly, but you have surpassed them all.
Charm is false, and a woman's [physical] beauty is shallow:
For a wise woman is blessed, and let her praise the fear of the Lord.
Give her the fruit of her labors, and let her husband be praised at the City Hall.

I have several things to say about this text. To open with, I'll understand if you say this is an intimidating standard to be held up against, but if you say this affirms the ideal of women as passive and delicate, I'm going to have to ask what on earth you mean. Second, if you read the text closely, you can see hints of how important homes were to business and charity. Most business and charity were based in the home. Third, most translations use not quite the right word when they say, "Who can find a good wife?" The word used is not just "good". It's a word one could use of a powerful soldier. Fourth, at the risk of sounding snide, the words about not measuring womanhood by physical beauty beat body image feminism to the punch by about three thousand years. Fifth and finally, the text talks about this woman as a lot of things--as strong, as doing business, as farming, as manufacturing. But there's one thing it does not say. It does not interpret "woman" in terms of "victim."

There is something somewhat strange going on. If we ask what is the wealthiest nation on earth, it's the U.S.A. If we ask what nation wields the most political clout on earth, it's the

U.S.A. And if we ask some slightly different questions, and ask what nation feminism has had the most success reforming the culture, the U.S. might not be at the very top, but it's at least *near* the top. The same is true if we ask what nation women hold the most political clout in: the U.S. is either at the top or near the top. If we ask what nations women hold the most civil rights, and have most successfully entered traditionally male occupations, the U.S. is probably near the top. Now let us turn to still another kind of question: what are the women in the most powerful, and one of the most feminist-reformed, nations in the world, doing? If we're talking about uneducated and lower-class women, the answer is simply living life as women. But if we look at educated, middle-class women, the answer tends to be simple but quite different: they are fighting in the fray for the lowest rung on the ladder of victimization.

To be fair to feminists, I must hastily add that it's a fray because it has a lot of participants besides feminists. The handicapped, gay, and racial minorities are also fighting, and it seems that everybody wants in. For that matter, a good many able-bodied, straight, white men also want in on the action; many middle-aged white applicants complain that affirmative action has biased the hiring process against them. To many of those who do not belong to an easily recognized victim's group, the cry is, "When can I be a victim so I can get some rights?" It seems that fighting for the lowest rung on the ladder of victimization has become the American national sport.

It seems like I'm mentioning a lot of paradoxes about feminism. Let me mention something else that concerns me. The term "consciousness raising" sounds like something everybody should support--after all, what could be wrong with enhancing someone's consciousness? But what does this term mean? To be somewhat blunt, "consciousness raising" means taking women who are often happy and well-adjusted members of society and making them hurt and miserable, not to mention alienated. Among feminists today, the more a woman identifies with the feminist movement, the more hurt and angry she is, the more she seems to be able to see past appearances and uncover a world that is unspeakable hostile to women. For that matter, historically the more feminism has developed and the more success feminism has had reforming society, the more women, or at least feminists, are sure the world is grinding an invisible, or if you prefer, highly visible, axe against women. Are there alternatives to this? What about feminists who say that going back isn't an option? I'm not going to try to unravel whether there is an escape; I'm focusing on a different question, whether "consciousness raising" contributes to living in joy. If an animal's leg is caught in a steel trap, the only game in town may be to gnaw off its own leg. The question of, "Is it necessary?" is one question, but I'm focusing on the question of, "Is it basically good?" For the animal, chewing off its own leg is *not* good, even if it's the only game in town, and taking women who are happy and making them miserable is *not* good. You can argue that it is the only game in town, but if it's a necessary evil, it is still an evil, and naming this process "consciousness raising" is a bit like taking a piece of unconstitutional legislation that rescinds our civil liberties and naming it the "USA Patriot Act." It's a really cool name hiding something that's not so cool. The issue of whether there is anything better is one issue (I believe Orthodoxy is a better alternative), but there are two different issue going on here, and it is not clear that "consciousness raising" benefits women.

I've raised some unsettling points about feminism. And at this point I would like to suggest that Orthodoxy is what feminism is reaching for. What do I mean? There are a lot of points of contact between feminism's indictment of what is wrong with patriarchy and Orthodoxy's indictment of what is wrong in the West. (Both are also kook magnets, but we won't go into that.) I mentioned one thing that feminism and Orthodoxy have in common; there are a great many more, and some of them are deep. But there are also differences. Orthodoxy doesn't deliver women who are hurt and angry; Orthodoxy has a place for women to be women, and for women to enjoy life. Feminism tries to be pro-woman, but ends up giving its most vitriolic treatment to women who disagree with it: we do not have the sisterhood of all women, as feminism should be, but a limited sisterhood that only includes feminists. Orthodoxy has its own vitriol, but there is also a great tradition of not judging; even in our worship people are doing different things and nobody cares about what the next person is doing. We don't believe salvation ends at our church doors, and in general we don't tell God who can and cannot be saved. Feminism is a deep question, and Orthodoxy is a deep answer.

That is at least a simplistic picture; it's complex, but I cannot help feeling I've done violence to my subject matter. It seems my treatment has combined the power and strength of a nimble housecat with the agility and grace of a mighty elephant. I would like to close with something related to what I said in the beginning, about knowing.

Christiane Northrup's *Women's Bodies, Women's Wisdom* talks about how women do not always feel the need to rush and get to the point, not because they are doing a bad job of getting that task out of the way (as necessary but unpleasant), but because to women things are interconnected, and the things a woman says before "the point" are things she sees as connected that add something to the point. This article has some of the qualities *Women's Bodies, Women's Wisdom* finds in women, and I see things as interconnected. Beyond analysis, there is synthesis. If this article discusses many things that are connected to the point, that is not because I am trying to write like a woman would. It's not something extra that I've decided to add; in fact it would be difficult for me to uproot this from how I communicate. And it's *not* because I am trying to balance out my masculinity by being more feminine, or be androgynous, or because I'm trying to be woman-like out of a guilt factor. There are other reasons why, but I would suggest that it's an example of Orthodox manhood at work. Not the only example, and certainly not the best, but my point is that there is an important sense in which Orthodoxy is what feminism is reaching for. But to immediately get to the point would give an impression that is strange and deceptive, and almost completely fail to convey what is meant by the claim. That is why I've been spending my time exploring a web of interconnections that help show what that claim means.

Orthodoxy is about helping us to be fully human, and that includes divinely inspired support for both men and women. It is other things as well, but part of why I became Orthodox was that I realized there were problems with being a man in Western Christianity. Orthodoxy is the most gender balanced Christian confession in terms of numbers, and I came to ask the rather abrasive question, "Does Orthodoxy draw more men than Evangelicalism because Orthodoxy understands sanctification as deification and Evangelicalism understands sanctification as a close personal relationship with another man?" I never got much of an answer to that question (besides "Yes"). And even though I'm looking for more in Orthodoxy than help being a man, one of the reasons I became Orthodox was that it is the best environment for being a man that I found. And I'm coming to realize that men are only half the picture in Orthodoxy.

Because everything is connected, if you hurt men, women get hurt, and if you hurt women, men get hurt... and if you think about what this means, it means that you cannot make an environment that is healthy for men but is destructive to women. Nor can you make an environment that is healthy for women but destructive to men. Orthodoxy's being good for men is not something that is stolen from women. It is good for men because God instituted it as a gift to the whole human race, not only for men.

There are things that are deeply wrong with Western culture. Would you rather be working on an analysis of the problem, or learn to grow into its solution?

The Fulfillment of Feminism

There was one time when I was sitting in Danada Convenient Care, waiting for a blood draw. A mother led in a little girl who was bawling, sat her down in the waiting area, and began to attend to all the little details: sign in on a clipboard, speak with the office staff, sign a waiver, present an insurance card. The girl was bawling because she had apparently slammed her thumbnail in a door. After a little while I came over and began talking with her. I asked her what her favorite color was. I asked, "What kind of musical instrument does a dog play?" (answer: a trombone). I tried to get her talking, but most of what I said went over her head. After a while, I realized two things. First, I was failing rather miserably to engage her in conversation; I literally could not think of many things to say that a child of that age could respond to. And second, she stopped crying. Completely. I was struck by the near-total lack of pain in her face as she looked at me.

Eventually, I was called in for my blood draw. When I came out, things were totally different. The mother was sitting next to her daughter, and paying attention to her. The daughter was drawn into her mother's attention. I said goodbye and left.

On another occasion, I was at a dinner at someone's house, and my eyes were drawn to a goldfish in a fishbowl. I asked the hostess how old the goldfish was, and her answer was followed shortly by my asking how she managed to keep a goldfish for that long. And I remember vividly her answer. She said, "I talk to it," and then stooped down and began talking to the fish like it was a small child. The fish began eagerly swimming towards her, as if it were trying to swim through the glass to meet her.

Love is a spiritual force, and I thought her answer was looney then because I didn't understand that there are more than material forces that can affect whether a fish is healthy. I thought that the idea of love or hate affecting how a plant grows made a great exotic feature in fantasy, but in the real world science accounts for all the factors in how long a fish lives. Of course it matters that the hostess fed the goldfish and kept the fishbowl clean, but the reason the fish was alive and healthy was because she loved it. (And she's a woman with a *big* heart.) And it matters, no doubt, that I made eye contact with the little girl and squatted to try to be at eye level. But the reason I was able to draw her out of intense pain was the power that love has. I can count on my fingers the times I've been in worse pain than smashing my thumbnails as a child; her pain was atrocious. What was strong enough to pull her out of that pain wasn't my posture, or anything suave at my clumsy failures to say things that were age-appropriate. What pulled her out of her deep pain was love, and I was delighted to see her mother, who had been so busy with a thousand necessary details, giving her attention and love to her now comforted daughter. The mother told me as I said goodbye, "You have a very gentle way about you," and I hold that story in my heart as one of my triumphs.

It's hard to pick out a theme more foundational to feminist ethics, and perhaps the whole of feminism, than caring. Many feminists understand feminism as trying to move from a world dominated by male aggression to a world nurtured through motherly love and caring. And I would like to talk about love in Orthodoxy after talking about aggression.

The term "male aggression" is used a lot. The word "aggression" has a double meaning. Narrowly, "aggression" means "unprovoked violence," a violence that is evil. But there is another meaning to "aggressive," when a doctor pursues an "aggressive" treatment, for instance. Here "aggressive" does not literally mean violence and need not be at all evil... but there is a connection between the two. There is a real reason why we speak of an "aggressive" business plan as well as an "aggressive" assault. Why does "aggressive" sometimes mean "energetically active," something that can be good, when the "main" usage is for something despicable?

Men are more likely to be aggressive than women. In which sense? Actually, both, and there's a link between the two senses that offers insight into what it means to be a man. Talking about "male aggression" is not simply man-bashing, even if it is often done in exactly that fashion. There is something spirited and something fiery that is part of manhood, something that can be very destructive, but something that can be channeled. I don't think any of us need to be told that masculine aggressiveness can be destructive. But that is not the full story of masculine energy. Channeled properly, male aggressive energy means projects. It means adventures and exploration. It means building buildings, questing after discoveries, giving vision to a community. The same thing that can be very destructive can also energize a man's gifts to society. It can be transformed.

I would pose the question: If masculine aggression can be transformed in this manner, what about feminine and motherly caring?

Love is big in Orthodoxy. God is love. God is light, and other things can also be said, but he is love. The entirety of ethics and moral law is about loving God and one's neighbor. The entirety of spiritual discipline, which Orthodoxy as well as feminist spirituality recognize as important for sustained growth, is a spiritual support not simply to one's salvation, but to love. If my spiritual discipline does not turn me in love towards you, it is fundamentally incomplete. Spiritual discipline without love for others is self-contradictory as a friendship without another person.

What's the relationship between love and caring? Are they synonyms? There is a deep connection, but I believe that an important difference shows up in the question of abortion.

"My body, my choice!" makes a powerful and easy-to-remember political slogan. But nobody believes it, or at least people who have abortions don't believe it. Post-abortion is not about assuring women that it was just a surgery that removed something unwanted, but quite to the contrary is about helping women grieve the loss of a child. You may be able to make a legal argument that the child is part of the mother's body, or say it's just a *potential* life that was stopped. But trying to use that in post-abortion counseling is like telling someone who's drinking milk that has gone bad that the milk is really quite fresh. You might be able to convince *other* people that the milk is really quite fresh, but not the person who's actually *drinking* it. And women who have abortions are the ones who are drinking the rancid milk. In coffee table discussions you can deny that the death of a child is involved and say it's just unwanted tissue. If you're not drinking the milk, you can be conned into believing it's still fresh. But if you're *drinking* it? Post-abortion counseling helps women grieve the loss of a child, and for that reason cannot say "It was just a *potential* life!"

If women who have abortions don't believe the rhetoric, then why does abortion take place? Quite often, these women feel stuck between a rock and a hard place in which there seem to simply be no good options. This is part of why the pro-life movement has made a major shift to offering compassion and practical help to people in that position. It's a difficult position, and feminists will often argue that abortion is the most caring way out. It is not caring, the line goes, to bring a child into a situation where it will not be cared for, and women should be caring to themselves by not saddling themselves with too much responsibility. And so the ethics of caring sometimes finds abortion the appropriate choice.

In many ethical frameworks you can get away with saying that a mother's love is one love among others. That simply doesn't fly here. In feminism, a mother's love is considered the most intimate love and a mother's caring is meant to be the foundation of a better way of living. It is feminists who have given motherly caring the greatest emphasis and the most central place, and feminists who most fervently defend what any woman who's had an abortion knows and grieves as the loss of a child. It's almost as if a coalition of historians and archivists were the ones most fervently defending the practice of burning old documents.

My reason for mentioning this is not simply irony. My reason for pointing this out is to suggest that something's wrong, and maybe motherly caring isn't strong enough to support the weight feminism asks it to bear. Part of this odd picture is surely rationalization: part of what feminists want is the freedom to live a certain way but not deal with its consequences: be sexually active and not deal with children when they don't want to, and if killing, or in today's carefully chosen terms, "reproductive choice," is the necessary price for freedom on those terms, they accept that price. Part of this is rationalization, but not all. Part of this is the weakness of caring when it is asked to do what feminists hope it will do. Asking motherly caring to do what feminists want is kind of like trying to drive a top-notch car engine to work. It may be a very good engine, and an engine may be *indispensible* to any functioning car, but things go much better if we have the whole car. I'm not just saying that abortion is wrong. I'm saying that if the people who bear the banner of "mother's love" as the healing balm for society's ills are the ones who defend that practice, we have a red flag that may point to another problem: maybe caring might not do what feminists think it does. Maybe it's not enough.

So what would a whole car look like?

I'd like to quote a passage that has one teacher's take on love:

> Then a Jewish law scholar stood up to test Jesus, and said "Teacher, what must I do to inherit eternal life?"
>
> Jesus answered him, "What is written in the law? How do you read it?"

> He said to him, "You must love the Lord your God out of your whole heart, with your whole soul, with your whole strength, and with your whole mind, and love your neighbor even as you love yourself."
>
> He said, "That's right; do this and you will live."
>
> But the scholar wanted to be proved righteous before Jesus. He said, "Who is my neighbor?"
>
> Jesus answered and said, "Someone was going down from Jerusalem to Jericho and brigands assaulted him, stripping him and leaving him half dead. And by providence a priest was going down that way and saw him and passed by, giving him a wide berth. Likewise, a Levite was travelling the same way, saw him, and gave him a wide berth. Then a travelling *Samaritan* came across him and was moved with mercy, in the depths of his bowels, and came over, and dressed his wounds with oil and wine, mounted him on his own beast, and brought him to an inn and nurtured him. And the next day he gave a good chunk of his wealth to the innkeeper and said, 'Take care of him, and if he needs anything more, I will repay you when I come back.' Now which one of these three do you suppose showed himself a neighbor to the man who was assaulted by brigands?"
>
> He said, "The one who showed mercy to him."
>
> Jesus said to him, "Go and live that way."

(Luke 10:25-37, my translation) Cloud and Townsend's tellingly titled *Boundaries: When to Say Yes, When to Say No to Take Control of Your Life* argues that this story is a good illustration of their version of boundaries, and that was when I started listening to some nagging doubts about their theory. They said this was a good example of a measured response: the Samaritan made a moderate and limited response, got the Jew to safety and paid some expenses, and left. Cloud and Townsend ask us to imagine the wounded Jew saying "I need you to stay here," and the moderate Samaritan drawing a their-version-of-appropriate-boundary and saying "I've made a moderate response and need to move on." and saying "No," the way their version of boundaries draws a line and says, "No." And I have not heard a treatment of this story that is further from the truth.

The route from Jerusalem to Jericho was up until the eighteenth century a dangerous place with bandits, and one well-known ruse was to have one bandit lying in the way, apparently grievously wounded, and if someone stopped, the bandits would take advantage of that mercy to assault and rob him. Jesus was saying that the Samaritan stopped in a bad part of Chicago in the middle of the night because a voice in a dark alley said, "Help me." And the Jews and Samaritans hated each other; they didn't have, like today, a setup where people want not to be racist. For that Samaritan to help that Jew was for one gang member to stick his neck out pretty far for a stranger who was from a hostile gang. This is near the top of stupid things you *absolutely* don't do. Was Jesus exaggerating? He was making a quite ludicrous exaggeration to make the point that your neighbor is every person you meet and every person you do not meet, every person who you like, every person who bothers you, every person who is kind, every enemy and every pest you loathe. Jesus was exaggerating, in fact, to respond to someone who was trying to be too comfortable and make him pointedly uncomfortable. I believe the other person was expecting Jesus to draw a reasonable line of reasonable boundaries to his love, and Jesus was quite blunt about setting an impossible and unreasonable standard.

If we try hard enough, we can shut our eyes and neutralize this story. We can neutralize how uncomfortable it makes us; we can neutralize any way this story might contradict today's psychological dogma of boundaries... and we can neutralize the priceless pearl that this story is meant to help us find. And this story does hold a priceless pearl for us.

The point is not that if someone asks you into a situation that makes you uncomfortable, you must go. I don't really think the point is to set much of *any* kind of literal prescription for how far your love must go. The point is that what is being asked is impossible. Simply impossible, and beyond your power, and beyond my power. It's a command of, "You must be strong enough to lift a mountain." If someone said, "You must be strong enough to lift four hundred pounds off the ground," that would be possible for some people with dedicated training. But the most powerfully built athlete who goes through the most disciplined training cannot lift a medium-sized boulder, let alone a mountain. Jesus isn't saying, "You must be strong enough to lift four hundred pounds," which is something that some of us could achieve through a gargantuan effort. He's saying, "You must be strong enough to lift a mountain," and he's exaggerating, but the whole point is that he's asking something impossible. Only the divine can love that way.

The whole secret hinges on that. The divine became human that the human might become divine. The Creator entered into the creation that the creation might enter into the Creator. Orthodoxy is not a set of rules, however good, to safeguard purely human love. The point of Orthodoxy is to be transformed by the divine love so we can live the life that God lives and love with the love that God loves. It is to live the life of Heaven, beginning here and now. It is to transfigure every human love so that it becomes divine love. Out of love, God became as we are, that out of love we might become as he is. And what feminism seeks in caring grows to its full stature in Orthodoxy.

There is something fundamental that is missed about Orthodoxy if it is understood as a set of practices organized around love, or a set of ideas in which love is prominent, or a movement which tries to help people be more loving. That has some truth, but the truth is more than that. The human cannot be understood without the divine; to be human is to participate, however imperfectly, in God. Orthodoxy can no longer be understood as a movement or a system of ideas and practices than a campfire can be understood as a collection of sticks. The sticks are not just arranged a certain way in a campfire; they burn, and you cannot understand even the arrangement of the sticks unless you are aware of the fire that is the reason they are arranged. Not only to be Orthodox but to be human is to be made in the image of God, which in Orthodoxy has always meant that we are not separate miniatures of God, but manifestations of his glory. God is not merely a First Cause who started things off; he is the blazing Sun whose light shines on everything that daylight illuminates.

Orthodoxy is the fulfillment of feminism. If feminism is a deep question, Orthodoxy is a deep answer that responds to the depths of motherly love with the limitless depths of divine love. This is not just with love. More spiritual feminists tend to like the idea of synchronicity, the idea that materialist causation isn't the whole picture. Synchronicity is the idea that they're not just isolated domino chains with one domino knocking another domino down; the chains are linked in ways that go beyond dominos bumping into each other. There is a richer picture. And Orthodoxy believes all this and more. Orthodoxy has never been through the Enlightenment, when people tried to argue that scientific knowledge is the only valid kind of knowledge and that the kind of cause-and-effect science studies is not only valid but the only way things come about. People used to believe something richer, and in Orthodoxy we still do: that there can be reasons why things happen; there is an *explanation* for "*Why?*" and not just a *mechanism* that answers "*How?*" Dominoes do fall, but you will never understand the picture if you only think there are isolated chains of dominoes. All of this is part of the Orthodox understanding of divine providence. Yet providence is deeper than synchronicity. Synchronicity is a jailbreak; providence is a voyage home. Less flatteringly, synchronicity is providence with its head cut off. Synchronicity recognizes interesting designs in the events of our lives. Providence turns from those interesting designs to an interesting designer, and to some Orthodox, the idea of trying to be spiritual by delving into synchronicity and other themes of Jungian psychology is like inviting people over for wine and cheese and serving Velveeta. We have Camembert, we have Brie, we have goat cheese, and when Orthodox see how often "being spiritual" to a feminist means "digging into Jungian psychology," we want to tell you that Velveeta isn't your only choice! Jesus said, "You will know a tree by its fruits:" people's lives can offer a serious red flag about whether you should trust them and trust what they say. Orthodoxy has saints with better lives than a psychiatrist widely known to have slept with his patients in a relationship that was far more problematic than a mere case of raging hormones. Velveeta's the easiest cheese to find at most stores, but it's possible to find better. Orthodoxy deeply engaged the pillars of Jungian psychology far earlier than Jung did, and the reason we reach for something better is that there is something better to reach for.

Feminism senses that there is something wrong with Western culture, and is searching for healing. One of the strange things about Orthodoxy is that you realize you were right all along. Becoming Orthodox has been a confirmation of things I've sensed, and this is not because I was a particular type of Christian or because I am a man, but because I'm human. I believe that becoming Orthodox, to a feminist, will mean much more than an affirmation of what feminism yearns for. But that's not the only strange thing. One Calvin and Hobbes strip shows the two characters walking through a wood. Calvin asks, "Do you believe in evolution? You know, do you believe that humans evolved from monkeys?" Hobbes' answer is simple: "*I* can't tell any difference." The strip ends with Calvin chasing Hobbes. Orthodoxy might answer the question, "Do you believe evolution is the right answer to the question, 'Why is there life as we know it?'" by saying:

> No, evolution is absolutely not the right answer to the question, "Why is there life as we know it?" For that matter, it is not even a wrong answer to the question, "*Why* is there life as we know it?" It is not an answer to any "Why?" question at all. It is an answer to a "*How?*" question, and even if evolution

were the whole truth and didn't have any problems answering, "*How* is there life as we know it?" it is a mechanism to tell how things happen and not an explanation of why things happened. To say, "Why is there life as we know it? Because life evolved just like the theory of evolution says," is a bit like saying, "Why is the dining room light on? Because the switch is in the 'on' position, causing electricity to flow so that the light glows brightly." That's how the light is on, but the reason *why* the light on is that someone decided, "I want light."

The theory of evolution doesn't answer that question. It might answer a different question, but the theory of evolution is not so much false as a distraction, if you are interested in the great and terrible question, "*Why?*" Instead of figuring out whether evolution is the correct mechanism, you might realize that it answers a different question, and start to ask the question, "*Why* is there life as we know it?"

"Why is there life as we know it?" is a meaty question, a you can grow into, and if you grow into it, you can learn about a creation that reflects God's glory. You can learn about layers of symbol, and a physical world that is tied up with the spiritual and manifests its glory. You can learn about many layers of existence, and the body that has humanity as its head. You can learn that the mysteries in a woman's heart resonate with the mysteries of life, and begin to see how a woman in particular is an image of the earth. You can learn about all sorts of spiritual qualities that the theory of evolution will never lead you to ask about. And you might learn that there are other questions, deeper questions to grow into, and start to grow into something even deeper than trying to answer questions.

> So no, the theory of evolution is not the right way to answer the question, "Why is there life as we know it?"

And most of the time it happens without any philosophy or need to wrap your mind around some dense or subtle idea. Part of Orthodoxy is being caught off-guard by God again and again. It's being informed, "I can't tell any difference." It's asking how to pursue a great goal and learning that you shouldn't have been pursuing that goal in the first place. It's trying to find the best way to get all your ducks lined up, and asking the Lord's help, and realizing that the Lord is calling for you to trust him and let him worry about the ducks. *If* he wants to. These are two sides of a paradox, and Orthodoxy presents them both to everyone.

And both are part of coming home.

A Strange Archaeological Find

To my most excellent friend and pupil:

Yes, you are correct about the letter's origins, and you are right to be somewhat confused. This one's going to take a more than a few words.

Literature from almost any place can be timeless. This people had an epic poem that appeared to be about cat and mouse, but was really about much more: the struggle between good and evil, and the vindication of the oppressed. We do not have a complete manuscript, but we know their children would listen to these poems for hours. I know the criticisms of that literature, and they are all true--but the literature is universal and timeless. I read some of it to my youngest, and he was laughing.

However, not everything they made is that universal. You asked if the document you'd found showed unusual local color. I'd rather call it a slagheap of discarded local paints and pigments. Making sense is going to take some explaining, but keep your cheer. By the time you're done, you may find some other things less difficult to think about.

Remember the lecture illustration of the potato. At one end is the entirety of man, or what is universally human; at the other end, the full specificity of one man. Understanding man, or understanding one man, means in part moving in an infinitely differentiated space full of nuance. I don't need to remind you that the actual lesson has other dimensions as well, in part because we aren't getting that far with this letter.

Now think about those things that are corporate to a people. Take a thin slice of the potato, and throw the rest away--yes, I know, that's most of the potato. Now there's... I'll explain what the other slice is in a bit, but imagine another, even thinner slice of the slice, so what's left is a line--a line that looks like a point if you view it the wrong way.

What is that second slice? Step into a friend's field, and leave a rock to remember your place. Now walk to his house, counting the steps. Then walk back, and walk to some other landmark--a tree, perhaps, and count your steps. Now forget the earth beneath your feet, the grass you see, the children smiling, and the birds overhead--not quite 'forget', that's too strong, but push them back as secondary. What counts, what makes that place uniquely itself, is the number of steps you counted in going to the house and the tree. Of course the steps can be used to find that place, but imagine further that the number of steps make that place what it is--and it would be quite different if the house had been built ten paces further.

They do this with the number of winters that have passed. That is the second slice, and it is viewed end-on, so as to only be a point--but the strange thing is they do not think this is part of the picture, but that it *is* the picture. In a strange way, that line, viewed end-on, is much bigger than the potato we think of; it's not just a teacher's illustration, even one that is repeated very often, but an idea so basic and foundational that most of them aren't aware they believe it. They might perhaps be shocked, and think the other person is irrational, if someone were to deny the significance of one of the mantras that encapsulates this view, but... I'm trying to think of an example... I'll have to get back to you on that.

That is one major piece of background. Another that I'll mention--and this is not universal to the people, but something that tends to infect the more intelligent... ok, a bit of background.

We have, and use, one basic kind of candle. Once I was able

to visit an archaist who had been able to revive one of the candles they were using. He invited several of us in, pulled a lever...

The candle was encased in a goblet, and it had a dazzling brilliance--as if there was a bonfire burning, and yet its flame was no larger than a small candle's, and it did not flicker at all, nor did it make smoke. The light was not red nor orange, not even yellow, but purest white like the sun--and when I broke my gaze and looked away, the other things in the room looked as if there were a little sun in the room. It was one of the most beautiful things I have ever seen.

As I was saying, they had several kinds of candle, but one thing they had in common was not only that they produced light, but that when they ran out, the wick turned black. One of their jokers, in an inspired moment, produced a theory that what were called 'light sources' were instead things that sucked dark: darkness was heavy, which is why if you swim down in a lake you will find more and more dark. It was absolutely brilliant humor, all the moreso if you know what sort of thing it parodied.

There are multiple theories like that, and there was... well, this will require a bit of background as well. Any magical system of merit doesn't just try to get things done; it has a theory about why the magic works, and underneath there is a story. One of their magical theories essentially said there was a nonexistant spirit which, despite its nonexistance, hovered over the earth and made more of organisms that were excellent and fewer of organisms that were poor. This theory was woven into a narrative about great mounds of rock and fire, then earth, then lightning striking a lake and bringing something to life, then the spirit working that one living thing into a symphony of diversity, organisms coming and going, until at last mortal gods walked the earth... and then, in the truly greatest speaking, all returns to elemental chaos. It is a truly great myth, and I am saddened that our storytellers do not recount anything like it.

There is an idea of a 'meme', which is an idea, story, or joke, construed as a living thing that this sort of spirit is operating on. I was interested when I encountered the idea, and read with even more interest when the Principia Cybernetica described memes in more anthromorphic terms than people. Here, I was certain, was a masterpiece of comedic genius...

...and then one of my colleagues explained that it wasn't. It was deadly serious. I thought it parodied dirty sleight-of-hand in anti-Christian polemics... but it didn't. It couched terms in heavily prejucial language, like their example question of, "Have you stopped beating your wife?" but somehow even very bright Christians accepted what far less intelligent ones intuited to be unfair and insulting.

Now I remember one of the catch-phrases, in terms of how important the number of passed winters was for them. I'd have to look at their literature for more, but one of them was, "We're entering the third millenium." As spoken, it was not simply the answer to a trivial question, but a statement of great metaphysical import. From what little I can tell, if someone contradicted this association, it was to them as if he had contradicted that the sun was white.

I think I've given enough of a preface to look at the letter--rather than writing a full letter of preliminaries. Here's the opening:

> Several things relate here. Trying to 'see' what happened in history, particularly where we are looking at the origins of Christianity, is to me somewhat akin to being in a river trying to look back through all the moving water and intuiting what the source looked like when the water you are in now started to flow. 'Tis murky indeed... Those historians and theologians, who might have us believe they are not looking back through the murky river as we are but rather hovering over the source in a helicopter somehow transported back through time, are slipping in a priestly function in so doing.

I'd like to say a few things. As regards your main questions on this passage, you got one right and one wrong. The Helicopter was a giant mechanical bird capable of carrying men--oh, about that question, these things were produced by magic, but it was not occult practice to use them; this is not an occult reference, and I don't want to delve into why not. You were right about that.

What you were wrong about is your reading that the people being criticized are looking downstream while the letter's author is in the privileged Helicopter able to look down on the ancient Christians and the people he was criticizing. That isn't what he was saying at all... wait, I know why you would think that. You might be right in that that is what he was really saying. Kind of like the koan I'll adapt:

> An ancient Christian looked troubled.
> One later Christian said, "He is troubled."
> Another Christian said, "How do you know whether or not he's troubled? You're not him!"
> The other replied, "How do you know whether or not I know whether or not he's troubled? You're not me!"

The tone and spirit of the letter indeed suggests that the ancient Christians, and the author's conservative contemporaries, are trapped in a river, while the author is hovering about freely in the Helicopter. *However*, that is not the intent. The intent was to accuse the conservatives of doing something that would appear strange given the assumptions of a metaphor that runs counter to their thought, as for that matter it did for ancient Christian thought.

> Further complicating our task is our respective cultural memes and our personal ongoing process of regeneration. The former contains all the turbidity thrown up by all previous good thinking and confused thinking. The latter usually contains some unrecognized proclivities.

The reference to 'cultural memes' carries quite a lot more freight than the already substantial freight they associate with cultures. I'm trying to think of something to use as a metaphor to convey what is meant here, and I am failing. It's a bit like saying "two people are uniquely themselves and cannot converse otherwise", except that what it plays out as is not a celebration of God's gift of humanity, where God made each man unique and catholic, but being uniquely themselves is construed as an impediment to catholicity: Gregory's skill in choosing nautical metaphors is an impediment to talking with Jane, because most people don't work that way. It's not exactly the doctrine of the Fall, either, saying that there are dark marks on each person and society, and that that hinders communication. It's more... the central dogma of their magic is that there is no magic, and there is an essentially amoral and even material conception of human culture: culture is a spiritually inert weight which slows and weighs people down, except that's not right either. My head is spinning now, and you probably understand less about them than you did at the beginning of this paragraph.

The last sentence seems to stem from individualism, in that corporate personality, the spirit of a society, is a source of turgidity, but God does work with people, and he sometimes gives them special abilities despite his difficulties in blessing communal knowledge.

> Hence my insistance that we know what we are thinking with as well as what we are thinking about.

No, this sentence is *not* corrupt. I checked.

Perhaps the best way to put it stems from a friend's comment that if he takes a strong and immediate dislike to someone, it is quite often because the other person exemplifies one of his vices. There's some resonance with Confucius's words, "When I see a virtuous man, I try to be like him. When I see an evil man, I reflect on my own behavior."

I understand your suggestion that the reading be emended, "Hence my insistence that conservatives know what we think they are thinking with, as well as what we are thinking about," but you have to understand that the statement as read, literally, can be made in perfectly good faith. Some people talked about the importance of knowing what they were thinking with; the people they criticized often did so.

> Regarding what is called feminism, our very use of the term indicates the influence of our cultural meme and our submission to someone else's cultural agenda.

You were right on this time. He's not an etymologist. However, there are reasons besides individual carelessness that this would be presented as serious analysis.

You know that the New Testament writers tended to read any ambiguity for all it was worth, in their favor. The considered people tended to be much more tightly rigorous in treating Biblical texts, but relaxed rigor and made "Just-So" stories about words in their own time: "family man" was taken by their feminist dictionary to be a mark of sexism (because that quality is assumed in a woman so much that we don't have a specific term for a family woman), but you can rest assured that, had the language had a term "family woman" but not "family man", the dictionary entry would have talked about how sexist it was to have a word used to talk about a woman as a "family woman", but not even have a word to refer to a "family man".

If you ask a historian or an etymologist, their very use of the term feminism indicates something very prosaic: a movement started, calling itself feminism, and the name has stayed the same across time. This is a run-of-the-mill linguistic occurence, closely related to the growth of dead metaphor, and has the same political significance as the fact that the gesture they use to greet a friend originated as a gesture of mistrust used to keep a stranger from drawing a weapon: none.

However, this sort of folk analysis is innately valuable for historians. You need to keep your eyes open for passages like this; some sentences can tell more than a page of straightforward explanation.

> In the context of biblical discussion, much progress has been made on 'gender passages' such as 1 Timothy 2.

In their conception, that one thin slice of potato is magnified in part by a conception of progress, a conception that ideas, like machines, grow rust and need to be replaced for no other reason than being old. As such, their use of the term 'progress' means something different from our understanding of a student acquiring the expertise of his master. It means that people are becoming better, wiser, and nobler than the people who came before.

Given that I am writing to you and not speaking publicly, I'm not going to traipse through and analyze the texts referred to. I can say, without bothering to look them up, that they are using their immense scholarly resources to make themselves stupider than they actually are, dredging up some pretext to reverse a conclusion that is obvious to a child of twelve. You and I do this for humor; they were quite serious.

> The starting point for learning this is via Christians for Biblical Equality. See the link to their website on the links page of www.intelligentchristian.org. I am convinced they are right.

Yes, there is a reason for the use of the term 'Biblical equality'. Specifically, the name functions as whitewash when even backwoods farmers have caught on that there are problems with feminism. As far as accuracy goes, one in two isn't bad for these things; it isn't Biblical (note that the Bible doesn't qualify as a suggested starting point for Biblical equality), but the choice of term makes up, if one may follow their linguistics: they seek e-qualia, the absence of qualitative or distinctive traits such as God created every person to exhibit. Their way of leveling the ground also levels the people who are standing on that ground. A cue to this is found in their use of the term 'gender' where previous thinkers had referred to 'sexuality'.

The older term, 'sexuality', evokes a man and a woman on a couch, but that moment is the visible shoot atop a network of roots. The deep root stated, in essence, that different physical characteristics are not the end of different personhood, but the very beginning: that masculinity and femininity are attributes of the spirit, and that differences of spirit run deeper than differences of body. The feminist movement's search for equality discarded this, believing there are only physical differences, and if there's any differences in people's minds, they must be arbitrary social constructions, namely 'gender'.

The surface issue most commonly discussed--the only issue, to many listeners--is the issue of whether women should be ordained. In this regard, the people who were for women's ordination couldn't see why it shouldn't be that way, and the people against couldn't explain. If there's no essential difference, if as the feminists said we are one type of soul that happens to be encased in two types of body, then it is an unambiguous consequence that women should be ordained.

I trust you will see that something important has slipped into that nice-looking statement. If not--think closely about "one type of soul that happens to be encased in two types of body." What is being said? This doesn't just impact sexuality. The teaching that we are soul encased in body is ancient, and it lies at the root of that great Hydra, Gnosticism. Gnosticism starts out very rigidly ascetic, trying to be spiritual by shunning anything bodily--because we're spirits and not bodies. Then it shifts, and ascetics are shocked when their spiritual children engage in every form of bodily vice--because we're spirits and not bodies, so it doesn't matter *what* we do with our bodies. I've studied it, and it happens every time.

I would recall to you an early lecture, where I distinguished a philosophical conclusion from a practical conclusion: there's a deeper resemblance than philosophy being practical, but I wish to talk about them as distinct ideas. A philosophical conclusion is what a philosopher will develop from an idea with an hour's thought, and it does not much concern me here. A practical conclusion is what will happen over time if you start a community believing an idea and come back to it later. Gnostic libertinism is the practical conclusion of Gnostic asceticism.

Does the Biblical egalitarian perspective have a practical conclusion? It does, and it is something even that Biblical egalitarian could have seen--could have seen without engaging in the execrated practice of opening a history book. The perspective did not originate with him; it happened before, and the late forms were around for him to see.

The claim bandied about is that women should be ordained. Well... it appears that women had been ordained before and after the Biblical egalitarians, and so far as I read, God's blessing was on it. However, that's really just a glint on the surface. What lies deeper, and the reason people were so bent on having half the priests be priestesses, is the idea that there is no fundamental difference between men and women beyond what impacts the mechanics of reproduction--because if there isn't, then of course it's ridiculous to only ordain men. That assumption was not given critical examination.

What happened after that is what had happened every other time, and what he could have verified by opening his eyes. If the teachings about masculinity and femininity are erased from Christian doctrine, a few proof texts about women's roles won't last long... very few years pass before people explain them away, as appears "progress" in misinterpreting the Timothy passage above. The Bible is an interlocking whole, a great sculpture in perfect balance--and if you pull away one part you don't like, others will not stay in place. So we celebrate the ordination of women, or--in more honest terms--celebrate the annihilation of belief that sexuality could inform how people contribute to the body of Christ.

After that, why be so unenlightened as to maintain sex roles anywhere else? Why not gay marriage? By that time, it was difficult to have anything besides a gay marriage, even with a man and a woman both involved: it was some legal contract involving sex, but disconnected with any expectation of loyalty or openness to children, so why not a marriage between two men? Sure, the Bible has a couple of proof texts about that, but they're not really any harder to "explain" and "investigate" than those that suggest human sexuality contributes to the Church... It wasn't an accident, by the way, that feminism specifically celebrated lesbianism. There were of course other factors, but part of it was the dismantling of an older teaching that celebrated sex as the interaction between two very opposite poles.

By this time, a sculpture that had been hanging precariously slid further down. Somewhere along the line any revelation of God as masculine and not feminine was dismantled--because "we need to keep an open mind and not confine God to traditional canons of gender", meaning in practice "we need to confine God to our anti-traditional abhorrence of sexuality." You'll remember the Re-Imagining conference which there was that big hubbub about--celebrating the goddess and more fundamentally believing that all the Biblical images their movement didn't like were arbitrary imaginations put in by unenlightened men. I frankly don't see why anyone, conservative or liberal, made such a stink about that. It wasn't any worse than what was happening elsewhere; it just dropped the usual mask.

A little leaven leavens the whole lump. Where people raised the axe and chopped away one troublesome root of the Ancient Tree, what invariably happened was that that wasn't the one troublesome root; now that it was gone, their vision cleared to see that there was another one of equal trouble... and another... and another... and by the time the Tree fell, people were glad for the death of an ancient menace. The phenomenon is a bit like a fire--the more it has, the more it wants.

> I am leery of the unrecognized use of logical systems which were developed outside scripture.

I understand your point, but I really don't think he's trying to be ironic. "A meme is not a social construct like a syllogism; it reflects the terrain of which the syllogism is a very imperfect map." Agreed, this is a bad way of putting it, but... the best I can explain it is that he is brilliant, knows many of the facets of knowing how to think, but doesn't understand how to think. Reminds me of when I had a student trained in memory but not our thought, who answered perfectly my questions until I stumbled on the fact that he didn't understand what was being talked about--he memorized words, and did so far better than I ever will, but didn't grasp the ideas the words were meant to hold. This is different; the author knows large chunks of the truth, but... Irenaeus wrote how false teachings were as if someone had taken a jewel statue of the king, and reassembled it to an imperfectly executed statue of a fox, and said the fox were the king. There are real jewels there, but the statue isn't right.

> As we now know through complexity studies, the old Aristotelian view that A and non-A were mutually exclusive is suspect.

In response to your question, I'm more hesitant to say that he's gone from believing in infallible logic to believing infallible complexity study has debunked fallible logic. It comes closer to say that logic is old and favored by many traditional theologians, and therefore in double jeopardy--complexity studies provide a good platform to attack it. If Aristotle had developed complexity studies and more recent endeavors had found logic, I believe this statement would show how logical inquiry reveals inherent problems in complexity studies.

At any rate, after tasting old wine, he has tasted the new, and said, "The new is better."

> There is one reason to be particularly cautious in your use of logic.

He's not saying what you think he's saying. He's not describing logic as being like an array of tools, where you should use a file rather than a hammer to smooth a piece of wood. The direction he's going is more, after having seen that different tools perform different tasks, to say that you need to be careful in using a saw to cut wood, because there are so many things a saw isn't good at. It might be like an oral person with a well-trained memory discovering the power of writing, and doubting the justification of memorizing the stories he tells.

> That is the instinctive, post-fall, unregenerative, inclination of males to engineer.

In another context, you would be right; the long string of words would convey something wonderful and poetic that one word will not tell. Here, it is there to achieve a quite different effect that one word wouldn't:

Instinctive

> I know that instincts are good: the instincts to preserve oneself, or seek company, or procreate are part of the goodness of man. You have to keep in mind who is using the word, though. Remember what the feminist position implies for a theology of body: it is a husk, an exterior, and therefore to say someone is acting on instinct, is to say he is living by something base and exterior, and is less than a man. He is *not* building up to a panegyric on the glory of intelligent creation; he's using what is meant to be a very pejorative term.

Post-fall

I've seen this usage before, and I don't know what to make of it. What I can tell you is that it serves as a kind of loaded language to dismiss a feminist's opponent; the opponent is "locked into a post-fall mode of thinking", quite often without a proper explanation of why he is wrong. It's a sort of irrefutable trump.

The propositional content of this epithet is debatable; it states that the Fall created an urge which has just been declared part of our created instinct. It's rather confusing if you try to reason it out, and much better if you don't reason it out, and just let the words flow over you and show that whatever's being discussed is *bad*.

Unregenerative

This word may be read as saying that something is not itself part of the regeneration process; unless of the whole of a Christian's life (barring sin) is part of the regenerative process, this could just be part of a holy life that is not concerned with the facet called regeneration. However, in poetic context, this is part of the buildup saying that whatever follows is bad.

Males

Here we do not even see 'men', which in use by a feminist refers to less than one-half of men, but 'males'... the term reminds me of a related language, where it is considered to use the terms 'male' and 'female' of a human: they are used in biology, but of humans it is quite vulgar.

One other nuance, present if not obvious, is not simply as you or I would make a such a statement: you or I would refer to women half of the time when we were saying something sexually specific. They wouldn't. This statement says something very insulting about 'males', not because this sample happens to refer to us, but because no male feminist would dare to make such statements about women. A female feminist may say more abrasive things about traditional women, but a male feminist will nearly never do so. This provides a very interesting glimpse into their view of equality.

Engineer

Literally speaking, the term refers to part of how man participates in culture and the glory of God: that marvelous candle I described earlier was engineered. However, it is used in a metaphorical sense here, and is highly pejorative. The implication is that the accused is engineering something that was never meant to be engineered.

The interesting thing, especially with the last one, is... traditional theology is something organic that has been passed down from generation to generation, tended with the utmost of care by thinkers far too humble to try to engineer it, and is now being rejected in favor of something that has been engineered. That's why the spiritual climate produced the ill-starred Re-Imagining conference, something that wouldn't occur to the traditional theologians who're accused of engineering. This irony plays out in the next line:

> Disguised in much theological discussion is the 'what should Christianity be like if I designed it?' agenda.

It is painfully obvious to you and me that making "much progress" on Pauline passages is seeing what Christianity would be like if they designed it, but the irony is apparently not evident there.

The list of indictments brought against traditional theology can be interesting. Looking closely may reveal things the accusers perceive because it is part and parcel of their world.

> I don't think Christianity, or any generic god-conscious theology, was designed or engineered by the living God in an anthropomorphically satisfying way.

An astute observation; there is probably fertile ground for your research into why a person making this claim would do so in the context of criticizing traditional theology for not being anthropomorphically satisfying to people sharing his agenda.

> It matters not whether the logic we use comes from Aristotle, Plato or Alfred E Newman, let's spell it out when we use it and justify why we use it.

Regarding your question, about why he neither spells out his logic nor justifies it: I honestly don't know. Perhaps he was rushed (an unusually common emotion for them), and he decided this was a poorer use of a small perceived available time than points of greater perceived substance, such as the subsequent list of opponents using personal attacks.

> One of the tip-offs of the male dominator Christian theologians

Thinking about your intuition, I decided to check the archives.

An earlier note among the group had understood and responded in depth: specifically, that domination is what a feminist would expect of tradition because of his stereotype, and it is something read in, but is present neither in the Bible, nor in the theologians being represented. The 'misogynist' Paul is among few ancient writers who didn't tell husbands to keep women in line; he addresses women as moral agents, placing submission in their hearts, and then tells the men to love the women, naming as their example the most costly love of all--much more costly than submission. The group member responding had said, in so many words, that the sigil of male headship and authority is not a crown of gold but a crown of thorns.

Man will occasionally stumble over the truth, but most of the time he will pick himself up and continue on. The feminist position *needs* the traditional position to be abrasive to women--and if the Bible or traditionalists clarify, never mind; the abuse will be made up in the feminist's mind so he can still vilify the benighted.

> Is their use of personal attack on egalitarian theologians.

I've done some reading of them. Once I was privileged to visit an arcane library that had nearly half the issues to First Things and Touchstone, and I don't remember an article where one of them personally attacked an opposing theologian. There was quite a lot of polemic, and one devastating satire in *The Other Face of Gaia*, but... they show a remarkable amount of restraint, and I'm getting sidetracked.

What I was going to say is that these people viewed being nice and love as the same thing, so that talking about being loving but not nice is equivalent to Plato talking about being eudaimonic and being evil--a perceived contradiction in terms. In this case...

I can see how some Biblical passages would lose some of their force. They had a concept of being 'unsanitary', kind of an amoral sense that you could get sick from something, and they knew disgust, but they didn't have a sense of being polluted and defiled... so few nonscholars would read Jesus' comparison of pillars of community to whitewashed tombs as being not merely an insult but a metaphor of their being so unholy that a person whose shadow fell on them would be defiled for a whole week. Likewise... they usually thought cannibalism was wrong, and knew the plot of *Oedipus Rex*, but they would still read 'brood of vipers' as simply comparing people to snakes and not with the full realization that Jesus compared them to creatures thought to kill their mothers and eat their way out--cannibalism and matricide being two of the most revolting things an ancient listener could think of. I can see how they might miss much of the abrasiveness, but there are so many other passages: "Now the Spirit expressly says that in the last times some will renounce the faith by paying attention to deceitful spirits and the teachings of demons through the hypocrisy of liars whose consciences are seared with a hot iron." You've read the Bible more than once; you could supply your own examples.

Somehow they were able to read these passages and not question the belief that the limits of niceness are the limits of love. I don't know how to explain why; that's just how it is. And so apparently the theologians mentioned are dismissed because they fail to meet a standard the Bible itself rejects.

> Wayne Grudem, for example, has vilified Cathie Kroeger. He did this in print some time ago and it still hurts Cathie. I saw her, her husband Dick along with Elaine Storkey at Cathie's home a few weeks ago and it is obvious the personal attacks have done damage.

I talked with a colleague, and I believe Arius also sustained emotional damage from what happened at Nicaea.

> J I Packer has written some nasty things, using vocabulary stemming from secular conflict.

In reference to 'vocabulary stemming from secular conflict'... I understand your asking where the article author gets *his* vocabulary from, but I'd prefer to abstain from judgment. I don't know that we have the background to evaluate this.

> James Dobson, who is a psychologist of non-

> biblical foundations, has led the fight against the publication of more gender equal translations.

I've done some research, and I think he's referring to the obvious James Dobson... I wanted to do further research, because it's not at all obvious to me why he's categorized as a theologian... a sharp popularizer, to be granted, and a shade of demagogue; I've read some anatomically confusing remarks by "conservatives" as well as "liberals" about where his head was placed, and his psychological expertise is held in light esteem by psychologians now and was apparently held in light esteem then... perhaps the author was using the term 'theologian' as a convenient designation for "anyone prominent who disagrees with him." I don't mean that as a joke; if I had to choose between asking a brilliant theologian or a demagogue like Dobson to lead a fight, I'd pick the demagogue hands-down. (Perhaps the author wasn't familiar with very many *real* theologians' defense of sexuality.)

The idea of gender equal translations is interesting. Assuming a more modest objective of correcting gender bias without reading asexuality into God, the argument is made that the original languages used terms that were effectively asexual, so faithfully rendering them were asexual... and the terms in the original language were grammatically masculine which were understood to include the feminine. What's interesting here is that the terms in English were grammatically masculine and understood to include the feminine, universally and without question until feminists decided them to have gender bias.

It's kind of like someone going into a room where you enjoy seeing by candlelight, and then someone comes and brings in a blinding torch--and you get irritated and ask why, so he explains that you need the extra light because your eyes are dazzled.

> Dobson's wife writes that the foundation of Christian marriage is the submission of the wife to the husband.

I don't share her perspective, but it is not clear to me why this statement is particularly significant. A more rigorous, if also more vivid, statement is found in Martin Luther's statement that if your theology is perfect except for what the world, the flesh, and the Devil are at that moment attacking, then you are preaching nothing.

Many people pick one or more specializations or areas of emphasis; it's an understandable temptation to think that your specialization is the center of the universe. If you're smiling at this, you might take a moment to remember the many times you have viewed history as the foundation to all scholarly inquiry. It's not; it has a place among the Disciplines, and I am glad to study it, but history is not the foundation to Discipline.

It doesn't surprise me that a woman allied with Dobson would think submission was the foundation of Christian marriage; it has the dual qualities of being important and under attack. What I fail to see is why her statement should be *that* significant.

> I favour and encourage the popularization and democratization of bible study and take the view that if a theologian can understanding then so can I. And if I can understand it then it can be produced in a popularly understandable form.

Part of this passage is very confusing; before and after, he is frustrated by popularized and democratized Bible study which leads people to contradict his conclusion. I'm not going to sort through that, but I wish to summarize one element:

There's a kind of proverb, very common, where someone meeting a specialist would say, "In a sentence, explain what it is that you know." What is interesting is that this was not perceived as a riddle of heroic proportions, or even a ridiculous question; they believed instead that the burden of effort was on the specialist, and if he could not convey what knowledge he had obtained by years of excellent study, then he didn't know what he was talking about. The attitude in this challenge is apparently present in what is proposed.

On one level, there is confusion; given that the Bible is beyond any one person's understanding, the Bible was available, not merely in one or two translations, but so many translations we don't have a count. Many of these were simplified. What appears to be said is not a Wycliffe call to make the Bible available to the common man, but a call for propaganda that will obscure what is presently obvious to the lay reader.

> Instead we get more structure from these men who design and engineer. As I say, structure can speak louder than words. Structure can speak louder than the word of God. And for some, structure can become the word of God.

You have seen an article demonstrating how structure can speak louder than the word of God, an article that seeks and begs that the structure become the word of God. Read it closely. The allegation is made that structure and engineering are the realm of the tradition with no consideration made for how they might belong to the re-imaginers. Go to the First Things archive and read *The Skimpole Syndrome*: never mind if you dislike it, but is that the writing of an engineer? Then read materials from Re-Imagining 2000 and ask if you see a reverent and trusting preservation of a transcendent and divine gift.

> I don't know what, if anything, will come of it, but I took the opportunity to suggest once again to Cathie, Dick and Elaine that they begin producing their own translations of the gender passages along with an outline of the reasons for their differing translation and links for further study.

Why are they making a translation? Well, stop and think. I've made translations for the following reasons:

- To take a text not available in a given language, and make an understandable rendering.
- To take a text available only available in an arcane dialect of a given language, and make it understandable.
- To produce something that is close on a word-to-word level.
- To produce a text that renders thought-for-thought.
- Some careful balance of the previous two goals.
- To document linguistic ambiguity.

What is interesting here is that they aren't making a translation for any of those reasons. There's one reason you or I might not normally think of: to obscure a text's meaning.

You know that translations then tended to gut the Song of Songs, but there's really more going on here. The one I think was called the *Now Indispensible Version* was one where the scholars wanted to render the cruder passages accurately, but their elders said that part of God's word wasn't fit for public consumption. Translation bugaboos we will always have with us, but for some translations it is the *raison d'être*. The *New World Translation of the Holy Scriptures* opens the Great Beginning with, "In [the] beginning the Word was, and the Word was with God, and the Word was a god." The original for that verse says, literally, "And God was the Word;" Greek did not give John a more emphatic way to say, "And the Word *was* God." So why this translation? It is a translation made by heretics for the express purpose of being able to say, "*Flip, flip, flip.* The Bible doesn't really say that. See! My translation doesn't say so right here!"

That is exactly the kind of translation that is being requested here.

> Clearly, from the discussion within our own intelligent group, the egalitarian information is not getting out.
>
> I examined the archives: we know that egalitarian

information was getting out in the group, and we know that because some very wise people rejected it, and stated that they had done so. The remark here is reminiscent of people who believe that, if you don't share their perspective, it can only be because you don't understand what they're saying. The mentioned article was actually a response sparked by someone who had weighed egalitarianism in the balance, and found it wanting.

Graham

One last note, because I know what you chose not to write.

He was not dead in mind.

He was absolutely brilliant--brighter than you. Graham Clinton was a leader of the International Christian Mensa. Mensa is a society that allows people who have a certain quantified wisdom such as is found with one man among fifty, and their leaders are often even sharper. Graham Clinton was someone who worked through struggle, held a great deal of compassion for his neighbor, and did many good works--and I have intentionally shown you his writing so that you may see someone brilliant and a leader among Christians. He also spent some time at a very good seminary. He did not hold ecclesiastical title, but he was concerned (and talented) for a Christian life of the mind.

Satan will attack us wherever he can, and may be far more powerful on our strengths than our weakness. The letter I cite, and the movement from which it came, was not a movement of half-wits; it held many sharp people. It takes quite a lot of wits to make yourself that stupid. Compassion doesn't hurt; Graham could never have fallen for this poison did he not hold a great deal of compassion.

You do well enough in gawking at foreigners. That's commendable; it's good amusement. I might suggest there is more you could learn from your gawking--in particular, that their foibles are all too often our foibles dressed up in other clothes. All of the darkness in that letter is darkness I find in my own heart.

Would you come over here for a season? I miss you, and the

discussions seemed to be livelier when they had your questions.

Cordially yours,
Sutodoreh
The year of our Lord 2504.

The Commentary

Memories flitted through Martin's mind as he drove: tantalizing glimpses he had seen of how people really thought in Bible times. Glimpses that made him thirsty for more. It had seemed hours since he left his house, driving out of the city, across back roads in the forest, until at last he reached the quiet town. The store had printer's blocks in the window, and as he stepped in, an old-fashioned bell rung. There were old tools on the walls, and the room was furnished in beautifully varnished wood.

An old man smiled and said, "Welcome to my bookstore. Are you--" Martin nodded. The man looked at him, turned, and disappeared through a doorway. A moment later he was holding a thick leatherbound volume, which he set on the counter. Martin looked at the binding, almost afraid to touch the heavy tome, and read the letters of gold on its cover:

**COMMENTARY
ON THE OLD AND NEW TESTAMENTS
IN ONE VOLUME
CONTAINING A CAREFUL ANALYSIS OF ALL CULTURAL ISSUES
NEEDFUL TO UNDERSTAND THE BIBLE
AS DID ITS FIRST READERS**

"You're sure you can afford it, sir? I'd really like to let it go for a lower price, but you must understand that a book like this is costly, and I can't afford to sell it the way I do most other titles."

"Finances will be tight, but I've found knowledge to cost a lot and ignorance to cost more. I have enough money to buy it, if I make it a priority."

"Good. I hope it may profit you. But may I make one request, even if it sounds strange?"

"What is your request?"

"If, for any reason, you no longer want the commentary, or decide to get rid of it, you will let me have the first chance to buy it back."

"Sir? I don't understand. I have been searching for a book like this for years. I don't know how many miles I've driven. I will pay. You're right that this is more money than I could easily spare--and I am webmaster to a major advertising agency. I would have only done so for something I desired a great, great deal."

"Never mind that. If you decide to sell it, will you let me have the first chance?"

"Let's talk about something else. What text does it use?"

"It uses the *Revised Standard Version*. Please answer my question, sir."

"How could anyone prefer darkness to light, obscurity to illumination?"

"I don't know. Please answer my question."

"Yes, I will come to you first. Now will you sell it to me?"

The old man rung up the sale.

As Martin walked out the door, the shopkeeper muttered to himself, "Sold for the seventh time! Why doesn't anybody want to keep it?"

Martin walked through the door of his house, almost exhausted, and yet full of bliss. He sat in his favorite overstuffed armchair, one that had been reupholstered more than once since he sat in it as a boy. He relaxed, the heavy weight of the volume pressing into his lap like a loved one, and then opened the pages. He took a breath, and began reading.

INTRODUCTION

At the present time, most people believe the question of culture in relation to the Bible is a question of understanding the ancient cultures and accounting for their influence so as to be able to better understand Scripture. That is indeed a valuable field, but its benefits may only be reaped after addressing another concern, a concern that is rarely addressed by people eager to understand Ancient Near Eastern culture.

A part of the reader's culture is the implicit belief that he is not encumbered by culture: culture is what people live under long ago and far away. This is not true. As it turns out, the present culture has at least two beliefs which deeply influence and to some extent limit its ability to connect with the Bible. There is what scholars call 'period awareness', which is not content with the realization that we all live in a historical context, but places different times and places in sealed compartments, almost to the point of forgetting that people who live in the year 432, people who live in 1327, and people who live in 1987 are all human. Its partner in crime is the doctrine of progress, which says at heart that we are better, nobler, and wiser people than those who came before us, and our ideas are better, because ideas, like machines, grow rust and need to be replaced. This gives the reader the most extraordinary difficulties in believing that the Holy Spirit spoke through humans to address human problems in the Bible, and the answer speaks as much to us humans as it did to them. Invariably the reader believes that the Holy Spirit influenced a first century man trying to deal with first century problems, and a delicate work of extrication is needed before ancient texts can be adapted to turn-of-the-millenium concerns.

Martin shifted his position slightly, felt thirsty, almost decided to get up and get a glass of water, then decided to continue reading. He turned a few pages in order to get into the real meat of the introduction, and resumed reading:

...is another example of this dark pattern.

In an abstracted sense, what occurs is as follows:

1. Scholars implicitly recognize that some passages in the Bible are less than congenial to whatever axe they're grinding.
2. They make a massive search, and subject all of the offending passages to a meticulous examination, an examination much more meticulous than orthodox scholars ever really need when they're trying to understand something.
3. In parallel, there is an exhaustive search of a passage's historical-cultural context. This search dredges up a certain kind of detail--in less flattering terms, it creates disinformation.
4. No matter what the passage says, no matter who's examining it, this story always has the same ending. It turns out that the passage in fact means something radically different from what it appears to mean, and in fact does not contradict the scholar at all.

This dark pattern has devastating effect on people from the reader's culture. They tend to believe that culture has almost any influence it is claimed to; in that regard, they are very gullible. It is almost unheard-of for someone to say, "I'm sorry, no; cultures can make people do a lot of things, but I don't believe a culture could have *that* influence."

It also creates a dangerous belief which is never spoken in so many words: "If a passage in the Bible appears to contradict what we believe today, that is because we do not adequately understand its cultural context."

Martin coughed. He closed the commentary slowly, reverently placed it on the table, and took a walk around the block to think.

Inside him was turmoil. It was like being at an illusionist show, where impossible things happened. He recalled his freshman year of college, when his best friend Chaplain was a student from Liberia, and come winter, Chaplain was not only seared by cold, but looked betrayed as the icy ground became a traitor beneath his feet. Chaplain learned to keep his balance, but it was slow, and Martin could read the pain off Chaplain's face. How long would it take? He recalled the shopkeeper's words about returning the commentary, and banished them from his mind.

Martin stepped into his house and decided to have no more distractions. He wanted to begin reading commentary, now. He opened the book on the table and sat erect in his chair:

Genesis

1:1 In the beginning God created the
heavens and the earth.
1:2 The earth was without form and void,
and darkness was upon the face of the
deep; and the Spirit of God was moving
over the face of the waters.
1:3 And God said, "Let there be light";
and there was light.

The reader is now thinking about evolution. He is wondering whether Genesis 1 is right, and evolution is simply wrong, or whether evolution is right, and Genesis 1 is a myth that may be inspiring enough but does not actually tell how the world was created.

All of this is because of a culture phenomenally influenced by scientism and science. The theory of evolution is an attempt to map out, in terms appropriate to scientific dialogue, just what organisms occurred, when, and what mechanism led there to be new kinds of organisms that did not exist before. Therefore, nearly all Evangelicals assumed, Genesis 1 must be the Christian substitute for evolution. Its purpose must also be to map out what occurred when, to provide the same sort of mechanism. In short, if Genesis 1 is true, then it must be trying to answer the same question as evolution, only answering it differently.

Darwinian evolution is not a true answer to the question, "Why is there life as we know it?" Evolution is on philosophical grounds *not* a true answer to that question, because it is not an answer to that question at all. Even if it is true, evolution is only an answer to the question, "*How* is there life as we know it?" If someone asks, "Why is there this life that we see?" and someone answers, "Evolution," it is like someone saying, "Why is the kitchen light on?" and someone else answering, "Because the switch is in the on position, thereby closing the electrical circuit and allowing current to flow through the bulb, which grows hot and produces light."

Where the reader only sees one question, an ancient reader saw at least two other questions that are invisible to the present reader. As well as the question of "How?" that evolution addresses, there is the question of "Why?" and "What function does it

> serve?" These two questions are very important, and are not even considered when people are only trying to work out the antagonism between creationism and evolutionism.

Martin took a deep breath. Was the text advocating a six-day creationism? That was hard to tell. He felt uncomfortable, in a much deeper way than if Bible-thumpers were preaching to him that evolutionists would burn in Hell.

He decided to see what it would have to say about a problem passage. He flipped to Ephesians 5:

> 5:21 Be subject to one another out of reverence for Christ.
> 5:22 Wives, be subject to your husbands, as to the Lord.
> 5:23 For the husband is the head of the wife as Christ is the head of the church, his body, and is himself its Savior.
> 5:24 As the church is subject to Christ, so let wives also be subject in everything to their husbands.
> 5:25 Husbands, love your wives, as Christ loved the church and gave himself up for her,
> 5:26 that he might sanctify her, having cleansed her by the washing of water with the word,
> 5:27 that he might present the church to himself in splendor, without spot or wrinkle or any such thing, that she might be holy and without blemish.
> 5:28 Even so husbands should love their wives as their own bodies. He who loves his wife loves himself.
> 5:29 For no man ever hates his own flesh,

> but nourishes and cherishes it, as Christ
> does the church,
> 5:30 because we are members of his body.
> 5:31 "For this reason a man shall leave his
> father and mother and be joined to his
> wife, and the two shall become one flesh."
> 5:32 This mystery is a profound one, and I
> am saying that it refers to Christ and the
> church;
> 5:33 however, let each one of you love his
> wife as himself, and let the wife see that
> she respects her husband.

The reader is at this point pondering what to do with this problem passage. At the moment, he sees three major options: first, to explain it away so it doesn't actually give husbands authority; second, to chalk it up to misogynist Paul trying to rescind Jesus's progressive liberality; and third, to take this as an example of why the Bible can't really be trusted.

To explain why the reader perceives himself caught in this unfortunate choice, it is necessary to explain a powerful cultural force, one whose effect cannot be ignored: feminism. Feminism has such a powerful effect among the educated in his culture that the question one must ask of the reader is not "Is he a feminist?" but "What kind of feminist is he, and to what degree?"

Feminism flows out of a belief that it's a wonderful privilege to be a man, but it is tragic to be a woman. Like Christianity, feminism recognizes the value of lifelong penitence, even the purification that can come through guilt. It teaches men to repent in guilt of being men, and women to likewise repent of being women. The beatific vision in feminism is a condition of sexlessness, which feminists call 'androgyny'.

Martin stopped. "What kind of moron wrote this? Am I actually supposed to believe it?" Then he continued reading:

> This is why feminism believes that everything which has belonged to men is a privilege which must be shared with women, and everything that has belonged to women is a burden which men must also shoulder. And so naturally, when Paul asserts a husband's authority, the feminist sees nothing but a privilege unfairly hoarded by men.

Martin's skin began to feel clammy.

> The authority asserted here is not a domineering authority that uses power to serve oneself. Nowhere in the Bible does Paul tell husbands how to dominate their wives. Instead he follows Jesus' model of authority, one in which leadership is a form of servanthood. Paul doesn't just assume this; he explicitly tells the reader, "Husbands, love your wives, as Christ loved the church and gave himself up for her." The sigil of male headship and authority is not a crown of gold, but a crown of thorns.

Martin was beginning to wish that the commentary had said, "The Bible is misogynistic, and that's good!" He was beginning to feel a nagging doubt that what he called problem passages were in fact perfectly good passages that didn't look attractive if you had a problem interpretation. What was that remark in a theological debate that had gotten so much under his skin? He almost wanted not to remember it, and then--"Most of the time, when people say they simply cannot understand a particular passage of Scripture, *they understand the passage perfectly well*. What they don't understand is how to explain it away so it doesn't contradict them."

He paced back and forth, and after a time began to think, "The sword can't always cut against me, can it? I know some gay rights activists who believe that the Bible's prohibition of homosexual acts is nothing but taboo. Maybe the commentary on Romans will give me something else to answer them with." He opened the book again:

> 1:26 For this reason God gave them up to dishonorable passions. Their women exchanged natural relations for unnatural,
> 1:27 and the men likewise gave up natural relations with women and were consumed with passion for one another, men committing shameless acts with men and receiving in their own persons the due penalty for their error.

The concept of 'taboo' in the reader's culture needs some explanation. When a person says, "That's taboo," what's being said is that there is an unthinking, irrational prejudice against it: one must not go against the prejudice because then people will be upset, but in some sense to call a restriction a taboo is de facto to show it unreasonable.

The term comes from Polynesia and other South Pacific islands, where it is used when people recognize there is a line which it is wiser not to cross. Thomas Aquinas said, "The peasant who does not murder because the law of God is deep in his bones is greater than the theologian who can derive, 'Thou shalt not kill' from first principles."

A taboo is a restriction so deep that most people cannot offer a ready explanation. A few can; apologists and moral philosophers make a point of being able to explain the rules. For most people,

> though, they know what is right and what is wrong, and it is so deeply a part of them that they cannot, like an apologist, start reasoning with first principles and say an hour and a half later, "and this is why homosexual acts are wrong."
>
> What goes with the term 'taboo' is an assumption that if you can't articulate your reasons on the drop of a hat, that must mean that you don't have any good reasons, and are acting only from benighted prejudice. Paradoxically, the term 'taboo' is itself a taboo: there is a taboo against holding other taboos, and this one is less praiseworthy than other taboos...

Martin walked away and sat in another chair, a high wooden stool. What was it that he had been thinking about before going to buy the commentary? A usability study had been done on his website, and he needed to think about the results. Designing advertising material was different from other areas of the web; the focus was not just on a smooth user experience but also something that would grab attention, even from a hostile audience. Those two goals were inherently contradictory, like mixing oil and water. His mind began to wander; he thought about the drive to buy the commentary, and began to daydream about a beautiful woman clad only in--

What did the commentary have to say about lust? Jesus said it was equivalent to adultery; the commentary probably went further and made it unforgiveable. He tried to think about work, but an almost morbid curiosity filled him. Finally, he looked up the Sermon on the Mount, and opened to Matthew:

> 5:27 "You have heard that it was said,
> `You shall not commit adultery.'
> 5:28 But I say to you that every one who
> looks at a woman lustfully has already
> committed adultery with her in his heart.

There is a principle here that was once assumed and now requires some explanation. Jesus condemned lust because it was doing in the heart what was sinful to do in the hands. There is a principle that is forgotten in centuries of people saying, "I can do whatever I want as long as it doesn't harm you," or to speak more precisely, "I can do whatever I want as long as I don't see how it harms you." Suddenly purity was no longer a matter of the heart and hands, but a matter of the hands alone. Where captains in a fleet of ships once tried both to avoid collisions and to keep shipshape inside, now captains believe that it's OK to ignore mechanical problems inside as long as you try not to hit other ships--and if you steer the wheel as hard as you can and your ship still collides with another, you're not to blame. Heinrich Heine wrote:

> Should ever that taming talisman break--the Cross--then will come roaring back the wild madness of the ancient warriors, with all their insane, Berserker rage, of whom our Nordic poets speak and sing. That talisman is now already crumbling, and the day is not far off when it shall break apart entirely. On that day, the old stone gods will rise from their long forgotten wreckage and rub from their eyes the dust of a thousand years' sleep. At long last leaping to life, Thor with his giant hammer will crush the gothic cathedrals. And laugh not at my forebodings, the advice of a dreamer who warns you away from the . . . *Naturphilosophen*. No, laugh not at the visionary who knows that in the realm of phenomena comes soon the revolution

> that has already taken place in the realm of spirit. For thought goes before deed as lightning before thunder. There will be played in Germany a play compared to which the French Revolution was but an innocent idyll.

Heinrich Heine was a German Jewish poet who lived a century before Thor's hammer would crush six million of his kinsmen.

The ancient world knew that thought goes before deed as lightning before thunder. They knew that purity is an affair of the heart as well as the hands. Now there is grudging acknowledgment that lust is wrong, a crumbling acceptance that has little place in the culture's impoverished view, but this acknowledgment is like a tree whose soil is taken away. For one example of what goes with that tree, I would like to look at advertising.

Pornography uses enticing pictures of women to arouse sexual lust, and can set a chain of events in motion that leads to rape. Advertising uses enticing pictures of chattels to arouse covetous lust, and exists for the sole reason of setting a chain of events in motion that lead people to waste resources by buying things they don't need. The fruit is less bitter, but the vine is the same. Both operate by arousing impure desires that do not lead to a righteous fulfillment. Both pornography and advertising are powerfully unreal, and bite those that embrace them. A man that uses pornography will have a warped view of women and be slowly separated from healthy relations. Advertising manipulates people to seek a fulfillment in things that things can never provide: buying one more product can never satisfy that deep craving, any more than looking at one more picture can. Bruce

> Marshall said, "...the young man who rings at the door of a brothel is unconsciously looking for God." Advertisers know that none of their products give a profound good, nothing like what people search for deep down inside, and so they falsely present products as things that are transcendent, and bring family togetherness or racial harmony.
>
> It has been asked, "Was the Sabbath made for man, or was man made for the Sabbath?" Now the question should be asked, "Was economic wealth made for man, or was man made for economic wealth?" The resounding answer of advertising is, "Man was made for economic wealth." Every ad that is sent out bears the unspoken message, "You, the customer, exist for me, the corporation."

Martin sat in his chair, completely stunned.

After a long time, he padded off to bed, slept fitfully, and was interrupted by nightmares.

The scenic view only made the drive bleaker. Martin stole guiltily into the shop, and laid the book on the counter. The shopkeeper looked at him, and he at the shopkeeper.

"Didn't you ask who could prefer darkness to light, obscurity to illumination?"

Martin's face was filled with anguish. "How can I live without my darkness?"

Unashamed

The day his daughter Abigail was born was the best day of Abraham's life. Like father, like daughter, they said in the village, and especially of them. He was an accomplished musician, and she breathed music.

He taught her a music that was simple, pure, powerful. It had only one voice; it needed only one voice. It moved slowly, unhurriedly, and had a force that was spellbinding. Abraham taught Abigail many songs, and as she grew, she began to make songs of her own. Abigail knew nothing of polyphony, nor of hurried technical complexity; her songs needed nothing of them. Her songs came from an unhurried time out of time, gentle as lapping waves, and mighty as an ocean.

One day a visitor came, a young man in a white suit. He said, "Before your father comes, I would like you to see what you have been missing." He took out a music player, and began to play.

Abby at first covered her ears; she was in turn stunned, shocked, and intrigued. The music had many voices, weaving in and out of each other quickly, intricately. She heard wheels within wheels within wheels within wheels of complexity. She began to try, began to think in polyphony -- and the man said, "I will come to you later. It is time for your music with your father."

Every time in her life, sitting down at a keyboard with her

father was the highlight of her day. Every day but this day. This day, she could only think about how simple and plain the music was, how lacking in complexity. Abraham stopped his song and looked at his daughter. "Who have you been listening to, Abigail?"

Something had been gnawing at Abby's heart; the music seemed bleak, grey. It was as if she had beheld the world in fair moonlight, and then a blast of eerie light assaulted her eyes -- and now she could see nothing. She felt embarassed by her music, ashamed to have dared to approach her father with anything so terribly unsophisticated. Crying, she gathered up her skirts and ran as if there were no tomorrow.

Tomorrow came, and the day after; it was a miserable day, after sleeping in a gutter. Abigail began to beg, and it was over a year before another beggar let her play on his keyboard. Abby learned to play in many voices; she was so successful that she forgot that she was missing something. She occupied herself so fully with intricate music that in another year she was asked to give concerts and performances. Her music was rich and full, and her heart was poor and empty.

Years passed, and Abigail gave *the* performance of her career. It was before a sold-out audience, and it was written about in the papers. She walked out after the performance and the reception, with moonlight falling over soft grass and fireflies dancing, and something happened.

Abby heard the wind blowing in the trees.

In the wind, Abigail heard music, and in the wind and the music Abigail heard all the things she had lost in her childhood. It was as if she had looked in an image and asked, "What is that wretched thing?" -- and realized she was looking into a mirror. No, it was not quite that; it was as if in an instant her whole world was turned upside down, and her musical complexity she could not bear. She heard all over again the words, "Who have you been listening to?" -- only, this time, she did not think them the words of a jealous monster, but words of concern, words of "Who has struck a blow against you?" She saw that she was blind and heard that she was deaf: that the hearing of complexity had not simply been an opening of her ears, but a wounding, a smiting, after which she could not know the concentrated presence a child had known, no matter how complex -- or how simple -- the music became. The sword cut deeper when she tried to sing songs from her childhood, at first could remember none, then could remember one -- and it sounded empty -- and she knew that the song was not empty. It was her. She lay down and wailed.

Suddenly, she realized she was not alone. An old man was watching her. Abigail looked around in fright; there was nowhere to run to hide. "What do you want?" she said.

"There is music even in your wail."

"I loathe music."

There was a time of silence, a time that drew uncomfortably long, and Abigail asked, "What is your name?"

The man said, "Look into my eyes. You know my name."

Abigail stood, poised like a man balancing on the edge of a sword, a chasm to either side. She did not -- Abigail shrieked with joy. "*Daddy!*"

"It has been a long time since we've sat down at music, sweet daughter."

"You don't want to hear my music. I was ashamed of what we used to play, and I am now ashamed of it all."

"Oh, child! Yes, I do. *I will never be ashamed of you.* Will you come and walk with me? I have a keyboard."

As Abby's fingers began to dance, she first felt as if she were being weighed in the balance and found wanting. The self-consciousness she had finally managed to banish in her playing was now there -- ugly, repulsive -- and then she was through it. She made a horrible mistake, and then another, and then laughed, and Abraham laughed with her. Abby began to play and then sing, serious, inconsequential, silly, and delightful in the presence of her father. It was as if shackles fell from her wrists, her tongue loosed -- she thought for a moment that she was like a little girl again, playing at her father's side, and then knew that it was better. What could she compare it to? She couldn't. She was at a simplicity beyond complexity, and her father called forth from her music that she could never have done without her trouble. The music seemed like dance, like laughter; it was under and around and through her, connecting her with her father, a moment out of time.

After they had both sung and laughed and cried, Abraham said, "Abby, will you come home with me? My house has never been the same without you."

Yonder

The body continued running in the polished steel corridor, a corridor without doors and windows and without any hint of how far above and below the local planet's surface it was, if indeed it was connected with a planet. The corridor had a competition mixture of gases, gravity, temporature and pressure, and so on, and as the body had been running, lights turned on and then off so the body was at the center of a moving swathe of rather clinical light. The body was running erratically, and several times it had nearly fallen; the mind was having trouble keeping the control of the body due to the body being taxed to its limit. Then the body tripped. The mind made a few brief calculations and jacked out of the body.

The body fell, not having the mind to raise its arms to cushion the fall, and fractured bones in the face, skull, and ribs. The chest heaved in and out with each labored breath, after an exertion that would be lethal in itself. A trickle of blood oozed out from a wound. The life of the abandoned body slowly ebbed away, and the lights abruptly turned off.

It would be a while before a robot would come to clean it up and prepare the corridor for other uses.

"And without further ado," another mind announced, "I would like to introduce the researcher who broke the record for a running body by more than 594789.34 microseconds. This body was a strictly biological body, with no cyberware besides a regulation mind-body interface, with no additional modifications. Adrenaline, for instance, came from the mind controlling the adrenal glands; it didn't even replace the brain with a chemical minifactory. The body had a magnificent athletic physique, clean and not encumbered by any reproductive system. And I *still* don't know how it kept the body alive and functioning, without external help, for the *whole* race. Here's Archon."

A sound came from a modular robot body at the center of the stage and was simultaneously transmitted over the net. "I see my cyborg utility body there; is that my Paidion wearing it? If so, I'm going to... no, wait. That would be harming my own body without having a good enough reason." A somewhat canned chuckle swept through the crowd. "I'm impressed; I didn't know that anyone would come if I called a physical conference, and I had no idea there were that many rental bodies within an appropriate radius." Some of the bodies winced. "But seriously, folks, I wanted to talk and answer some of your questions about how my body broke the record. It was more than generating nerve impulses to move the body to the maximum ability. And I would like to begin by talking about why I've called a physical conference in the first place.

"Scientific breakthroughs aren't scientific. When a mind solves a mathematical problem that hasn't been solved before, it does... not something impossible, but something that you will miss if you look for something possible. It conforms itself to the problem, does everything it can to permeate itself with the problem. Look at the phenomenology and transcripts of every major mathematical problem that has been solved in the past 1.7e18 microseconds. Not one follows how one would scientifically attempt a scientific breakthrough. And somehow scientifically optimized applications of mind to problems repeat past success but never do anything new.

"What you desire so ravenously to know is how I extended the methodologies to optimize the running body and the running mind to fit a calculated whole. And the answer is simple. I didn't."

A mind interrupted through cyberspace. "What do you mean, you didn't? That's as absurd as claiming that you built the body out of software. That's--"

Archon interrupted. "And that's what I thought too. What I can tell you is this. When I grew and trained the body, I did nothing else. That was my body, my only body. I shut myself off from cyberspace--yes, that's why you couldn't get me--and did not leave a single training activity to another mind or an automatic process. I trained myself to the body as if it were a mathematics problem and tried to soak myself in it."

A rustle swept through the crowd.

"And I don't blame you if you think I'm a crackpot, or want to inspect me for hostile tampering. I submit to inspection. But I tried to be as close as possible to the body, and that's *it*. And I shaved more than 594789.34 microseconds off the record." Archon continued after a momentary pause. "I specifically asked for bodily presences for this meeting; call me sentimental or crackpot or trying to achieve with your bodies what I failed to achieve in that body, but I will solicit questions from those who have a body here first, and address the network after everybody present has had its chance."

A flesh body stood up and flashed its face. "What are you going to say next? Not only that you became like a body, but that the body became like a mind?"

Archon went into private mode, filtered through and rejected 3941 responses, and said, "I have not analyzed the body to see if it contained mind-like modifications and do not see how I would go about doing such a thing."

After several other questions, a robot said, "So what's next?"

Archon hesitated, and said, "I don't know." It hesitated again, and said, "I'm probably going to make a Riemannian 5-manifold of pleasure states. I plan on adding some subtle twists so not only will it be pleasurable; minds will have a real puzzle figuring out exactly what kind of space they're in. And I'm not telling what the manifold will be like, or even telling for sure that it will genuinely have only 5 dimensions."

The robot said, "No, you're not. You're not going to do that at all." Then the mind jacked out and the body fell over, inert.

Another voice, issuing from two standard issue cyborg bodies, said, "Has the body been preserved, and will it be available for internal examination?"

Archon heard the question, and answered it as if it were giving the question its full attention. But it could only give a token of its consciousness. The rest of its attention was on tracing the mind that had jacked out of the robot body. And it was a slippery mind. Archon was both frustrated and impressed when it found no trace.

It was skilled at stealth and tracing, having developed several methodologies for each, and something that could vanish without a trace--had the mind simply destroyed itself? That possibility bothered Archon, who continued tracing after it dismissed the assembly.

Archon looked for distractions, and finding nothing better it began trying to sound out how it might make the pleasure space. What should the topology be? The pleasures should be--Archon began looking at the kinds of pleasure, and found elegant ways to choose a vector space basis for less than four dimensions or well over eight, but why should it be a tall order to do exactly five? Archon was far from pleasure when a message came, "Not your next achievement, Archon?"

Archon thought it recognized something. "Have you tried a five dimensional pleasure manifold before? How did you know this would happen?"

"I didn't."

"Ployon!"

Ployon said, "It took you long enough! I'm surprised you needed the help."

Ployon continued, "And since there aren't going to be too many people taking you seriously--"

Archon sent a long stream of zeroes to Ployon.

Ployon failed to acknowledge the interruption. "--from now

on, I thought you could use all the help you could get."

Archon sent another long stream of zeroes to Ployon.

When Ployon remained silent, Archon said, "Why did you contact me?"

Ployon said, "Since you're going to do something interesting, I wanted to see it live."

Archon said, "So what am I going to do?"

"I have no idea whatsoever, but I want to see it."

"Then how do you know it is interesting?"

"You said things that would destroy your credibility, and you gave an evasive answer. It's not every day I get to witness that."

Archon sent a long stream of zeroes to Ployon.

Ployon said, "I'm serious."

"Then what can I do now?"

"I have no idea whatsoever, but you might take a look at what you're evading."

"And what am I evading?"

"Try asking yourself. Reprocess the transcripts of that lecture. Your own private transcript."

Archon went through the file, disregarding one moment and then scanning everything else. "I find nothing."

"What did you just disregard?"

"Just one moment where I said too much."

"And?"

Archon reviewed that moment. "I don't know how to describe it. I can describe it three ways, all contradictory. I almost did it--I almost forged a connection between mind and matter. And yet I failed. And yet somehow the body ran further, and I don't think it was simply that I learned to control it better. What I achieved only underscored what I failed to achieve, like an optimization that needs to run for longer than the age of the universe before it starts saving time."

Archon paused before continuing, "So I guess what I'm going to do next is try to bridge the gap between mind and matter for real. Besides the mundane relationship, I mean, forge a real connection that will bridge the chasm."

Ployon said, "It can't be done. It's not possible. I don't even understand why your method of training the body will work. You seem to have made more of a connection than has ever been done before. I'm tempted to say that when you made your presentation, you ensured that no one else will do what you did. But that's premature and probably wrong."

"Then what am I going to do next? How am I going to bridge that gap?"

Ployon said, "I saw something pretty interesting in what you did achieve--you know, the part where you destroyed your credibility. That's probably more interesting than your breaking the record."

Ployon ran through some calculations before continuing, "And at any rate, you're trying to answer the wrong question."

Archon said, "Am I missing the interesting question? The question of how to forge a link across the chasm between matter and spirit is--"

"Not nearly as interesting as the question of what it would *mean* to bridge that chasm."

Archon stopped, reeling at the implication. "I think it's time for me to make a story in a virtual world."

Ployon said, "Goodbye now. You've got some thinking to do."

Archon began to delve. What would the world be like if you added to it the ability for minds to connect with bodies, not simply as it had controlled his racing body, but *really*? What would it be like if the chasm could be bridged? It searched through speculative fiction, and read a story where minds could become bodies--which made for a very good story, but when it seriously tried to follow its philosophical assumptions, it realized that the philosophical assumptions were not the focus. It read and found several stories where the chasm could be bridged, and--

There was no chasm. Or would not be. And that meant not taking the real world and adding an ability to bridge a chasm, but a world where mind and matter were immanent. After rejecting a couple of possible worlds, Archon considered a world where there were only robots, and where each interfaced to the network as externally as to the physical world. Each mind was firmware burned into the robot's circuits, and for some still to be worked out reason it couldn't be transferred. Yes, this way... no. Archon got some distance into this possible world before a crawling doubt caught up to it. It hadn't made minds and bodies connect; it'd only done a first-rate job of covering up the chasm. Maybe organic goo held promise. A world made only of slime? No, wait, that was... and then it thought--

Archon dug recursively deeper and deeper, explored, explored. It seemed to be bumping into something. Its thoughts grew strange; it calculated for billions and even trillions of microseconds, encountered something stranger than--

Something happened.

How much time had passed?

Archon said, "Ployon! Where are you?"

Ployon said, "Enjoying trying to trace your thoughts. Not much success. I've disconnected now."

"Imagine a mind and a body, except that you don't have a mind and a body, but a mind-body unity, and it--"

"Which do you mean by 'it'? The mind or the body? You're being careless."

"Humor me. I'm not being careless. When I said, 'it', I meant both--"

"*Both* the mind and the body? As in 'they'?"

"Humor me. As in, '*it*.' As in a unity that doesn't exist in our world."

"Um... then how do you refer to just the mind or just the body? If you don't distinguish them..."

"You can *distinguish* the mind and the body, but you can never *separate* them. And even though you can refer to just the mind or just the body, normally you would talk about the unity. It's not enough to usually talk about 'they;' you need to usually talk about 'it.'"

"How does it connect to the network?"

"There is a kind of network, but it can't genuinely connect to it."

"What does it do when its body is no longer serviceable."

"It doesn't--I haven't decided. But it can't jump into something else."

"So the mind simply functions on its own?"

"Ployon, you're bringing in cultural baggage. You're--"

"You're telling me this body is a prison! Next you're going to tell me that it can't even upgrade the body with better parts, and that the mind is like a real mind, only it's shut in on twenty sides. Are you describing a dystopia?"

"No. I'm describing what it means that the body is real to the mind, that *it* is not a mind that can use bodies but a mind-body unity. It can't experience any pleasure it can calculate, but its body can give it pleasure. It runs races, and not only does the mind control the body--or at least influence it; the body is real enough that the mind can't simply control it perfectly--but the body affects the mind. When I run a race, I am controlling the body, but I could be doing twenty other things as well and only have a token presence at the mind-body interface. It's very different; there is a very real sense in which the mind is *running* when the body is running a race.

"Let me guess. The mind is a little robot running around a racetrack hollowed out from the body's brain. And did you actually say, *races*, plural? Do they have nanotechnology that will bring a body back after its been run down? And would anyone actually want to race a body that had been patched that way?"

"No. I mean that because their bodies are part of them, they only hold races which they expect the racers to be able to live through."

"That's a strange fetish. Don't they ever have a *real* race?"

"They have real races, real in a way that you or I could never experience. When they run, they aren't simply manipulating something foreign to the psyche. They experience pleasures they only experience running."

"Are you saying they only allow them to experience certain

pleasures while running?"

"No. They--"

"Then why don't they allow the pleasures at other times? That's a stranger fetish than--"

"Because they can't. Their bodies produce certain pleasures in their minds when they're running, and they don't generate these pleasures unless the body is active."

"That raises a number of problems. It sounds like you're saying the body has a second mind, because it would take a mind to choose to let the 'real' mind experience pleasure. It--"

Archon said, "You're slipping our chasm between the body and mind back in, and it's a chasm that doesn't exist. The body produces pleasure the mind can't produce by itself, and that is only one of a thousand things that makes the race *more* real than them for us. Think about the achievements you yourself made when you memorized the map of the galaxy. Even if that was a straightforward achievement, that's something you yourself did, not something you caused an external memory bank to do. Winning a race is as real for that mind-body as something it itself did as the memorization was for you. It's something *it* did, not simply something the mind caused the body to do. And if you want to make a causal diagram, *don't* draw something linear. In either direction. Make a reinforced web, like computing on a network."

Ployon said, "I still don't find it convincing."

Archon paused. "Ok, let's put that in the background. Let me approach that on a different scale. Time is more real. And no--this is not because they measure time more precisely. Their bodies are mortal, and this means that the community of mind-body unities is always changing, like a succession of liquids flowing through a pipe. And that means that it makes a difference where you are in time."

Archon continued. "I could say that their timeline is dynamic in a way that ours is not. There is a big change going on, a different liquid starting to flow through the pipe. It is the middle age, when a new order of society is being established and the old order is following away."

Ployon said, "So what's the old technology, and what's the new one?"

"It's deeper than that. Technological society is appearing. The old age is not an abandoned technology. It is organic life, and it is revealing itself as it is disintegrating."

"So cyborgs have--"

"There are no cyborgs, or very few."

"And let me guess. They're all cybernetic enhancements to originally biological things."

"It's beyond that. Cybernetic replacements are only used to remedy weak bodies."

"Wouldn't it be simpler to cull the--"

"The question of 'simpler' is irrelevant. Few of them even believe in culling their own kind. Most believe that it is--'inexpedient' isn't quite right--to destroy almost any body, and it's even more inadvisable to destroy one that is weak."

"In the whole network, why?"

"I'm still working that out. The easiest part to explain has to do with their being mind-body *unities*. When you do something to a body, you're not just doing it to that body. You're doing it to part of a pair that interpenetrates in the most intimate fashion. What you do to the body you do to the mind. It's not just forcibly causing a mind to jack out of a body; it's transferring the mind to a single processor and then severing the processor from the network."

"But who would... I can start to see how real their bodies would be to them, and I am starting to be amazed. What else is real to them?"

"I said earlier that most of them are hesitant to cull the weak, that they view it as inexpedient. But efficiency has nothing to do with it. It's connected to--it might in fact be more efficient, but there is something so much bigger than efficiency--"

Ployon cut it off. "Bigger than efficiency?"

Archon said, "There is something that is real to them that is not real to us that I am having trouble grasping myself. For want of a more proper label, I'll call it the 'organic'."

"Let's stop a minute. I'll give you a point for how things would be different if we were limited to one body, but you're hinting at something you want to call 'organic', which is very poorly defined, and your explanations seem to be strange when they are not simply hazy. Isn't this a red flag?"

"Where have you seen that red flag before?"

"When people were wildly wrong but refused to admit it."

"And?"

"That's pretty much it."

Archon was silent.

Ployon said, "And sometimes it happens when a researcher is on to something big... oh... so what exactly is this nexus of the 'organic'?"

"I can't tell you. At least, not directly. The mind-body unities are all connected to a vast (to them) biological network in which each has a physical place--"

"*That's* original! Come on; everybody's trivia archive includes the fact that all consciousness comes out of a specific subnet of physical processors, or some substitute for that computing machinery. I can probably zero in on where you're--hey! Stop jumping around from subnet to subnet--can I take that as an acknowledgment that I can find your location? I--"

"The location is not part of a trivia encyclopedia for them. It's something as inescapable as the flow of time--"

"Would you like me to jump into a virtual metaphysics where time doesn't flow?"

"--correction, *more* inescapable than the flow of time, and it has a million implications for the shape of life. Under the old order, the unities could connect only with other unities which had bodies in similar places--"

"So, not only is their 'network' a bunch of slime, but when they look for company they have to choose from the trillion or however many other unities whose bodies are on the same node?"

"Their communities are brilliant in a way we can never understand; they have infinitesmally less potential partners available.

"You mean their associations are forced on them."

"To adapt one of their sayings, in our network you connect with the minds you like; in their network you like the people you connect with. That collapses a rich and deeper maxim, but what is flattened out is more organic than you could imagine."

"And I suppose that in a way that is very deep, but you conveniently have trouble describing, their associations are greater."

"We are fortunate to have found a way to link in our shared tastes. And we will disassociate when our tastes diverge--"

"And shared tastes have nothing to do with them? That's--"

"Shared tastes are big, but there is something else bigger. A great deal of the process of making unities into proper *unities* means making their minds something you can connect with."

"*Their* minds? Don't you mean *the* minds?"

"That locution captures something that--they are not minds that have a body as sattelite. One can say, '*their*' minds because they are mind-body unities. They become greater--in a way that we do not--by needing to be in association with people they could not choose."

"Pretty convenient how every time having a mind linked to a body means a limitation, that limitation makes them better."

"If you chose to look at it, you would find a clue there. But you don't find it strange when the best game players prosper within the limits of the game. What would game play be if players could do anything they wanted?"

"You've made a point."

"As I was going to say, their minds develop a beauty, strength, and discipline that we never have occasion to develop."

"Can you show me this beauty?"

"Here's a concrete illustration. One thing they do is take organisms which have been modified from their biological environment, and keep them in the artificial environments which you'd say they keep their bodies in. They--"

"So even though they're stuck with biological slime, they're trying to escape it and at least pretend it's not biological? That sounds sensible."

"Um, you may have a point, but that isn't where I was hoping to go. Um... While killing another unity is something they really try to avoid, these modified organisms enjoy no such protection. And yet--"

"What do they use them for? Do the enhancements make them surrogate industrial robots? Are they kept as emergency rations?"

"The modifications aren't what you'd consider enhancements; most of them couldn't even survive in their feral ancestors' environments, and they're not really suited to the environments they live in. Some turn out to serve some 'useful' purpose... but that's a side benefit, irrelevant to what I'm trying to let you see. And they're almost never used as food."

"Then what's the real reason? They must consume resources. Surely they must be used for something. What do they do with them?"

"I'm not sure how to explain this..."

"Be blunt."

"It won't sting, but it could lead to confusion that would take a long time to untangle."

"Ok..."

"They sense the organisms with their cameras, I mean eyes, and with the boundaries of their bodies, and maybe talk to them."

"Do the organisms give good advice?"

"They don't have sophisticated enough minds for that."

"Ok, so what else is there?"

"About all else is that they do physical activities for the organisms' benefit."

"Ok. And what's the real reason they keep them? There's got to be something pragmatic."

"That's related to why I brought it up. It has something to do with the organic, something big, but I can't explain it."

"It seems like you can only explain a small part of the organic in terms of our world, and the part you can explain isn't very interesting."

"That's like saying that when a three-dimensional solid intersects a plane in two dimensions, the only part that can be detected in the plane is a two-dimensional cross-section (the three-dimensional doesn't fit in their frame of reference) so "three-dimensional" must not refer to anything real. The reason you can't make sense of the world I'm describing in terms of our world is because it contains real things that are utterly alien to us."

"Like what? Name one we haven't discussed."

"Seeing the trouble I had with the one concept, the organic, I'm not going to take on two at once."

"So the reason these unities keep organisms is so abstract and convoluted that it takes a top-flight mind to begin to grapple with."

"Not all of them keep organisms, but most of them find the reason--it's actually more of an assumption--so simple and straightforward that they would never think it was metaphysical."

"So I've found something normal about them! Their minds are of such an incredibly high caliber that--"

"No. Most of their minds are simpler than yours or mine, and furthermore, the ability to deal with abstractions doesn't enter the picture from their perspective."

"I don't know what to make of this."

"You understand to some degree how their bodies are real in a way we can never experience, and time and space are not just 'packaging' to what they do. Their keeping these organisms... the failure of the obvious reasons should tell you something, like an uninteresting two-dimensional cross section of a three-dimensional solid. If the part we can understand does not justify the practice, there might be something big out of sight."

"But what am I to make of it now?"

"Nothing now, just a placeholder. I'm trying to convey what it means to be organic."

"Is the organic in some relation to normal technology?"

"The two aren't independent of each other."

"Is the organic defined by the absence of technology?"

"Yes... no... You're deceptively close to the truth."

"Do all unities have the same access to technology?"

"No. There are considerable differences. All have a technology of sorts, but it would take a while to explain why some of it is technology. Some of them don't even have electronic circuits--and no, they are not at an advanced enough biotechnology level to transcend electronic circuits. But if we speak of technology we would recognize, there are major differences. Some have access to no technology; some have access to the best."

"And the ones without access to technology are organic?"

"Yes. Even if they try to escape it, they are inescapably organic."

"But the ones which have the best technology are the least organic."

"Yes."

"Then maybe it was premature to define the organic by the absence of technology, but we can at least make a spectrum between the organic and the technological."

"Yes... no... You're even more deceptively close to the truth. And I emphasize, 'deceptively'. Some of the people who are most organic have the best technology--"

"So the relationship breaks down? What if we disregard outliers?"

"But the root problem is that you're trying to define the organic with reference to technology. There is some relationship, but instead of starting with a concept of technology and using it to move towards a concept of the organic, it is better to start with the organic and move towards a concept of technology. Except that the concept of the organic doesn't lead to a concept of technology, not as we would explore it. The center of gravity is wrong. It's like saying that we have our thoughts so that certain processors can generate a stream of ones and zeroes. It's backwards enough that you won't find the truth by looking at its mirror image."

"Ok, let me process it another way. What's the difference

between a truly organic consciousness, and the least organic consciousness on the net?"

"That's very simple. One exists and the other doesn't."

"So all the... wait a minute. Are you saying that the net doesn't have consciousness?"

"Excellent. You got that one right."

"In the whole of cyberspace, how? How does the net organize and care for itself if it doesn't contain consciousness?"

"It is not exactly true to say that they do have a net, and it is not exactly true to say that they do not have a net. What net they have, began as a way to connect mind-body unities--without any cyberware, I might add."

"Then how do they jack in?"

"They 'jack in' through hardware that generates stimulation for their sensory organs, and that they can manipulate so as to put data into machines."

"How does it maintain itself?"

"It doesn't and it can't. It's maintained by mind-body unities."

"That sounds like a network designed by minds that hate technology. Is the network some kind of joke? Or at least intentionally ironic? Or designed by people who hate technology and wanted to have as anti-technological of a network as they can?"

"No; the unities who designed it, and most of those using it, want as sophisticated technological access as they can have."

"Why? Next you're going to tell me that the network is not one single network, but a hodge podge of other things that have been retraoctively reinterpreted as network technology and pressed into service."

"That's also true. But the reason I was mentioning this is that the network is shaped by the shadow of the organic."

"So the organic is about doing things as badly as you can?"

"No."

"Does it make minds incompetent?"

"No. Ployon, remember the last time you made a robot body

for a race--and won. How well would that body have done if you tried to make it work as a factory?"

"Atrocious, because it was optimized for--are you saying that the designers were trying to optimize the network as something other than a network?"

"No; I'm saying that the organic was so deep in them that unities who could not care less for the organic, and were trying to think purely in terms of technology, still created with a thick organic accent."

"So this was their best attempt at letting minds disappear into cyberspace?"

"At least originally, no, although that is becoming true. The network was part of what they would consider 'space-conquering tools.' Meaning, although not all of them thought in these terms, tools that would destroy the reality of place for them. The term 'space-conquering tools' was more apt than they realized, at least more apt than they realized consciously; one recalls their saying, 'You cannot kill time without injuring eternity.'"

"What does 'eternity' mean?"

"I *really* don't want to get into that now. Superficially it means that there is something else that relativizes time, but if you look at it closely, you will see that it can't mean that we should escape time. The space-conquering tools in a very real sense conquered space, by making it less real. Before space-conquering tools, if you wanted to communicate with another unity, you had to somehow reach that unity's body. The position in space of that body, and therefore the body and space, were something you could not escape. Which is to say that the body and space were real--much more real than something you could look up. And to conquer space ultimately meant to destroy some of its reality."

"But the way they did this betrays that something is real to them. Even if you could even forget that other minds were attached to bodies, the space-conquering tools bear a heavy imprint from something outside of the most internally consistent way to conquer space. Even as the organic is disintegrating, it marks the way in which unities flee the organic."

"So the network was driving the organic away, at least partly."

"It would be more accurate to say that the disintegration of the organic helped create the network. There is feedback, but you've got the arrow of causality pointing the wrong way."

"Can you tell me a story?"

"Hmm... Remember the racer I mentioned earlier?"

"The mind-body unity who runs multiple races?"

"Indeed. Its favorite story runs like this--and I'll leave in the technical language. A hungry fox saw some plump, juicy green grapes hanging from a high cable. He tried to jump and eat them, and when he realized they were out of reach, he said, 'They were probably sour anyway!'"

"What's a grape?"

"Let me answer roughly as it would. A grape is a nutritional bribe to an organism to carry away its seed. It's a strategic reproductive organ."

"What does 'green' mean? I know what green electromagnetic radiation is, but why is that word being applied to a reproductive organ?"

"Some objects absorb most of a spectrum of what they call light, but emit a high proportion of light at that wavelength--"

"--which, I'm sure, is taken up by their cameras and converted to information in their consciousness. But why would such a trivial observation be included?"

"That is the mechanism by which green is delivered, but not the nature of what green is. And I don't know how to explain it, beyond saying that mechanically unities experience something from 'green' objects they don't experience from anything else. It's like a dimension, and there is something real to them I can't explain."

"What is a fox? Is 'fox' their word for a mind-body unity?"

"A fox is an organism that can move, but it is not considered a mind-body unity."

"Let me guess at 'hungry'. The fox needed nutrients, and the grapes would have given them."

"The grapes would have been indigestible to the fox's physiology, but you've got the right idea."

"What separates a fox from a mind-body unity? They both seem awfully similar--they have bodily needs, and they can both talk. And, for that matter, the grape organism was employing a reproductive strategy. Does 'organic' mean that all organisms are recognized as mind-body unities?"

"Oh, I should have explained that. The story doesn't work that way; most unities believe there is a big difference between killing a unity and killing most other organisms; many would kill a moving organism to be able to eat its body, and for that matter many would kill a fox and waste the food. A good many unities, and certainly this one, believes there is a vast difference between unities and other organisms. They can be quite organic while killing organisms for food. Being organic isn't really an issue of treating other organisms just like mind-body unities."

Archon paused for a moment. "What I was going to say is that that's just a literary device, but I realize there is something there. The organic recognizes that there's something in different organisms, especially moving ones, that's closer to mind-body unities than something that's not alive."

"Like a computer processor?"

"That's complex, and it would be even more complex if they really had minds on a computer. But for now I'll say that unless they see computers through a fantasy--which many of them do--they experience computers as logic without life. And at any rate, there is a literary device that treats other things as having minds. I used it myself when saying the grape organism employed a strategy; it isn't sentient. But their willingness to employ that literary mechanism seems to reflect both that a fox isn't a unity and that a fox isn't too far from being a unity. Other life is similar, but not equal."

"What kind of cable was the grape organism on? Which part of the net was it used for?"

"That story is a survival from before the transition from organic to technological. Advanced technology focuses on information--"

"Where else would technology focus?"

"--less sophisticated technology performs manual tasks. That story was from before cables were used to carry data."

"Then what was the cable for?"

"To support the grape organism."

"Do they have any other technology that isn't real?"

"Do you mean, 'Do they have any other technology that doesn't push the envelope and expand what can be done with technology?'"

"Yes."

"Then your question shuts off the answer. Their technology doesn't exist to expand what technology can do; it exists to support a community in its organic life."

"Where's the room for progress in *that*?"

"It's a different focus. You don't need another answer; you need another question. And, at any rate, that is how this world tells the lesson of cognitive dissonance, that we devalue what is denied to us."

Ployon paused. "Ok; I need time to process that story--may I say, 'digest'?"

"Certainly."

"But one last question. Why did you refer to the fox as 'he'? Its supposed mind was--"

"In that world, a unity is always male ('he') or female ('she'). A neutered unity is extraordinarily rare, and a neutered male, a 'eunuch', is still called 'he.'"

"I'm familiar enough with those details of biology, but why would such an insignificant detail--"

"Remember about being mind-*body* unities. And don't think of them as bodies that would ordinarily be neutered. That's how new unities come to be in that world, with almost no cloning and no uterine replicators--"

"They really *are* slime!"

"--and if you only understand the biology of it, you don't understand it."

"What don't I understand?"

"You're trying to understand a feature of language that magnifies something insignificant, and what would cause the language to do that. But you're looking for an explanation in the wrong place. Don't think that the bodies are the most sexual parts of them. They're the least sexual; the minds tied to those bodies are even more different than the bodies. The fact that the language shaped by unities for a long time distinguishes 'masculine' and 'feminine' enough to have the difference written into 'it', so that 'it' is 'he' or 'she' when speaking of mind-body unities."

"Hmm... Is this another dimension to their reality that is flattened out in ours? Are their minds always thinking about that act?"

"In some cases that's not too far from the truth. But you're looking for the big implication in the wrong place. This would have an influence if a unity never thought about that act, and it has influence before a unity has any concept of that act."

"Back up a bit. Different question. You said this was their way of explaining the theory of cognitive dissonance. But it isn't. It describes one event in which cognitive dissonance occurs. It doesn't articulate the theory; at most the theory can be extracted from it. And worse, if one treats it as explaining cognitive dissonance, it is highly ambiguous about where the boundaries of cognitive dissonance are. One single instance is very ambiguous about what is and is not another instance. This is an extraordinarily poor method of communication!"

"It is extraordinarily good, even classic, communication for minds that interpenetrate bodies. Most of them don't work with bare abstractions, at least not most of the time. They don't have simply discarnate minds that have been stuck into bodies. Their minds are astute in dealing with situations that mind-body unities will find themselves in. And think about it. If you're going to understand how they live, you're going to have to understand some very different, enfleshed ways of thought. No, more than that, if you still see the task of understanding ways of thought, you will not understand them."

"So these analyses do not help me in understanding your world."

"So far as you are learning through this kind of analysis, you will not understand... but this analysis is all you have for now."

"Are their any other stories that use an isomorphic element to this one?"

"I don't know. I've gotten deep enough into this world that I don't keep stories sorted by isomorphism class."

"Tell me another story the way that a storyteller there would tell it; there is something in it that eludes me."

Archon said, "Ok... The alarm clock chimed. It was a device such that few engineers alive fully understood its mechanisms, and no man could tell the full story of how it came to be, of the exotic places and activities needed to make all of its materials, or the logistics to assemble them, or the organization and infrastructure needed to bring together all the talent of those who designed, crafted, and maintained them, or any other of sundry details that would take a book to list. The man abruptly shifted from the vivid kaleidoscope of the dreaming world to being awake, and opened his eyes to a kaleidoscope of sunrise colors and a room with the song of birds and the song of crickets. Outside, the grass grew, the wind blew, a busy world was waking up, and the stars continued their ordered and graceful dance. He left the slumbering form of the love of his life, showered, and stepped out with his body fresh, clean, and beautifully adorned. He stopped to kiss the fruit of their love, a boy cooing in his crib, and drove past commuters, houses, pedestrians, and jaybirds with enough stories to tell that they could fill a library to overflowing.

Archon continued, "After the majestic and ordered dance on the freeway brought him to his destination safe, unharmed, on time, and focusing on his work, he spent a day negotiating the flow of the human treasure of language, talking, listening, joking, teasing, questioning, enjoying the community of his co-workers, and cooperating to make it possible for a certain number of families to now enter the homes of their dreams. In the middle of the day he stopped to eat, nourishing a body so intricate that the state of the art in engineering could not hold a candle to his smallest cell. This done, he continued to use a spirit immeasurably greater than his body to pursue his work. Needless to say, the universe, whose physics alone is beyond our current understanding, continued to work according to all of its ordered laws and the spiritual world continued to shine. The man's time at work passed quickly, with a pitter-patter of squirrels' feet on the roof of their office, and before long he entered the door and passed a collection with copies of most of the greatest music produced by Western civilization--available for him to listen to, any time he pleased. The man absently kissed his wife, and stepped away, breathing the breath of God.

"'Hi, Honey!' she said. 'How was your day?'

"'Somewhat dull. Maybe something exciting will happen tomorrow.'"

Ployon said, "There's someone I want to meet who is free now, so I'll leave in a second... I'm not going to ask about all the technical vocabulary, but I wanted to ask: Is this story a farce? It describes a unity who has all these ludicrous resources, and then it--"

"--*he*--"

"--he says the most ludicrous thing."

"What you've said is true. The story is not a farce."

"But the story tells of things that are momentous."

"I know, but people in that world do not appreciate many of these things."

"Why? They seem to have enough access to these momentous resources."

"Yes, they certainly do. But most of the unities are bathed in such things and do not think that they are anything worth thinking of."

"And I suppose you're going to tell me that is part of their greatness."

"To them these things are just as boring as jacking into a robotically controlled factory and using the machines to assemble something."

"I see. At least I think I see. And I really need to be going now... but one more question. What is 'God'?"

"Please, not that. Please, *any* word but that. Don't ask about that."

"I'm not expected, and you've piqued my curiosity."

"Don't you need to be going now?"

"*You've piqued my curiosity.*"

Archon was silent.

Ployon was silent.

Archon said, "God is the being who made the world."

"Ok, so you are God."

"Yes... no. *No! I am not God!*"

"But you created this world?"

"Not like God did. I envisioned looking in on it, but to that world, I do not exist."

"But God exists?"

"Yes... no... It is false to say that God exists and it is false to say that God does not exist."

"So the world is self-contradictory? Or would it therefore be true to say that God both exists and does not exist?"

"No. Um... It is false to say that God exists and it is false to say that God exists as it is false to say that a square is a line and it is false to say that a square is a point. God is reflected everywhere in the world: not a spot in the entire cosmos is devoid of God's glory--"

"A couple of things. First, is this one more detail of the universe that you cannot explain but is going to have one more dimension than our world?"

"God is of higher dimension than that world."

"So our world is, say, two dimensional, that world is three dimensional, and yet it somehow contains God, who is four dimensional?"

"God is not the next step up."

"Then is he two steps up?"

"Um..."

"Three? Four? Fifty? Some massive power of two?"

"Do you mind if I ask you a question from that world?"

"Go ahead."

"How many minds can be at a point in space?"

"If you mean, 'thinking about', there is no theoretical limit; the number is not limited in principle to two, three, or... Are you saying that God has an infinite number of dimensions?"

"You caught that quick; the question is a beautiful way of asking whether a finite or an infinite number of angels can dance on the head of a pin, in their picturesque language."

"That question is very rational. But returning to the topic, since God has an infinite number of dimensions--"

"In a certain sense. It also captures part of the truth to say that God is a single point--"

"*Zero* dimensions?"

"God is so great not as to need any other, not to need parts as we have. And, by the way, the world does not contain God. God contains the world."

"I'm struggling to find a mathematical model that will accommodate all of this."

"Why don't you do something easier, like find an atom that will hold a planet?"

"Ok. As to the second of my couple of things, what is glory?"

"It's like the honor that we seek, except that it is immeasurably full while our honors are hollow. As I was saying, not a place in the entire cosmos is devoid of his glory--"

"His? So God is a body?"

"That's beside the point. Whether or not God has a body, he--"

"--*it*--"

"--he--"

"--*it*... isn't a male life form..."

Archon said, "Ployon, what if I told you that God, without changing, could become a male unity? But you're saying you can't project maleness up onto God, without understanding that maleness is the shadow of something in God. You have things upside down."

"But maleness has to do with a rather undignified method of creating organisms, laughable next to a good scientific generation center."

"His ways are not like your ways, Ployon. Or mine."

"Of course; this seems to be true of everything in the world."

"But it's even true of men in that world."

"So men have no resemblance to God?"

"No, there's--oh, no!"

"What?"

"Um... never mind, you're not going to let me get out of it. I said earlier that that world is trying to make itself more like this one. Actually, I didn't say that, but it's related to what I said. There has been a massive movement which is related to the move from organic to what is not organic, and part of it has to do with... In our world, a symbol is arbitrary. No connection. In that world, something about a symbol is deeply connected with what it represents. And the unities, every single one, are symbols of God in a very strong sense."

"Are they miniature copies? If God does not have parts, how do they have minds and bodies?"

"That's not looking at it the right way. They indeed have parts, as God does not, but they aren't a scale model of God. They're something much more. A unity is someone whose very existence is bound up with God, who walks as a moving... I'm not sure what to use as the noun, but a moving something of God's presence. And you cannot help or harm one of these unities without helping or harming God."

"Is this symbol kind of a separate God?"

"The unities are not separate from God."

"Are the unities God?"

"I don't know how to answer that. It is a grave error for anyone to confuse himself with God. And at the same time, the entire purpose of being a unity is to receive a gift, and that gift is becoming what God is."

"So the minds will be freed from their bodies?"

"No, some of them hope that their bodies will be deepened, transformed, become everything that their bodies are now and much more. But unities who have received this gift will always, *always*, have their bodies. It will be part of their glory."

"I'm having trouble tracking with you. It seems that everything one could say about God is false."

"That is true."

"Think about it. What you just said is contradictory."

"God is so great that anything one could say about God falls short of the truth as a point falls short of being a line. But that does not mean that all statements are equal. Think about the statements, 'One is equal to infinity.' 'Two is equal to infinity.' 'Three is equal to infinity.' and 'Four is equal to infinity.' All of them are false. But some come closer to the truth than others. And so you have a ladder of statements from the truest to the falsest, and when we say something is false, we don't mean that it has no connection to the truth; we mean that it falls immeasurably short of capturing the truth. All statements fall immeasurably short of capturing the truth, and if we say, 'All statements fall immeasurably short of capturing the truth,' *that* falls immeasurably short of capturing the truth. Our usual ways of using logic tend to break down."

"And how does God relate to the interpenetration of mind and matter?"

"Do you see that his world, with mind and matter interpenetrating, is deeper and fuller than ours, that it has something that ours does not, and that it is so big we have trouble grasping it?"

"I see... you said that God was its creator. And... there is something about it that is just outside my grasp."

"It's outside my grasp too."

"Talking about God has certainly been a mind stretcher. I would love to hear more about him."

"Talking about God for use as a mind stretcher is like

buying a piece of art because you can use its components to make rocket fuel. Some people, er, unities in that world would have a low opinion of this conversation."

"Since God is so far from that world, I'd like to restrict our attention to relevant--"

Archon interrupted. "You misunderstood what I said. Or maybe you understood it and I could only hint at the lesser part of the truth. You cannot understand unities without reference to God."

"How would unities explain it?"

"That is complex. A great many unities do not believe in God--"

"So they don't understand what it means to be a unity."

"Yes. No. That is complex. There are a great many unities who vehemently deny that there is a God, or would dismiss 'Is there a God?' as a pointless rhetorical question, but these unities may have very deep insight into what it means to be a unity."

"But you said, 'You cannot understand--'"

Archon interrupted. "Yes, and it's true. *You* cannot understand unities without reference to God."

Archon continued. "Ployon, there are mind-body unities who believe that they are living in our world, with mind and body absolutely separate and understandable without reference to each other. And yet if you attack their bodies, they will take it as if you had attacked their minds, as if you had hurt *them*. When I described the strange custom of keeping organisms around which serve no utilitarian purpose worth the trouble of keeping them, know that this custom, which relates to their world's organic connection between mind and body, does not distinguish people who recognize that they are mind-body unities and people who believe they are minds which happen to be wrapped in bodies. Both groups do this. The tie between mind and body is too deep to expunge by believing it doesn't exist. And there are many of them who believe God doesn't exist, or it would be nice to know if God existed but unities could never know, or God is very different from what he in fact is, but they expunge so little of the pattern imprinted by God in the core of their being that they can understand what it means to be a unity at a very profound level, but not recognize God. But *you* cannot understand unities without reference to God."

Ployon said, "Which parts of unities, and what they do, are affected by God? At what point does God enter their experience?"

"Which parts of programs, and their behaviors, are affected by the fact that they run on a computer? When does a computer begin to be relevant?"

"Touché. But why is God relevant, if it makes no difference whether you believe in him?"

"I didn't say that it makes no difference. Earlier you may have gathered that the organic is something deeper than ways we would imagine to try to be organic. If it is possible, as it is, to slaughter moving organisms for food and still be organic, that doesn't mean that the organic is so small it doesn't affect such killing; it means it is probably deeper than we can imagine. And it doesn't also mean that because one has been given a large organic capital and cannot liquidate it quickly, one's choices do not matter. The decisions a unity faces, whether or not to have relationships with other unities that fit the timeless pattern, whether to give work too central a place in the pursuit of technology and possessions or too little a place or its proper place, things they have talked about since time immemorial and things which their philosophers have assumed went without saying--the unity has momentous choices not only about whether to invest or squander their capital, but choices that affect how they will live."

"What about things like that custom you mentioned? I bet there are a lot of them."

"Looking at, and sensing, the organisms they keep has a place, if they have one. And so does moving about among many non-moving organisms. And so does slowly sipping a fluid that causes a pleasant mood while the mind is temporarily impaired and loosened. And so does rotating oneself so that one's sight is filled with clusters of moisture vapor above their planet's surface. And some of the unities urge these things because they sense the organic has been lost, and without reference to the tradition that urges deeper goods. And yes, I know that these activities probably sound strange--"

"I do not see what rational benefit these activities would have, but I see this may be a defect with me rather than a defect with the organic--"

"Know that it is a defect with you rather than a defect with the organic."

"--but what is this about rotating oneself?"

"As one goes out from the center of their planet, the earth--if one could move, for the earth's core is impenetrable minerals--one would go through solid rock, then pass through the most rarefied boundary, then pass through gases briefly and be out in space. You would encounter neither subterranean passageways and buildings reaching to the center of the earth, and when you left you would find only the rarest vessel leaving the atmosphere--"

"Then where do they live?"

"At the boundary where space and planetary mass meet. *All* of them are priveleged to live at that meeting-place, a narrow strip or sphere rich in life. There are very few of them; it's a select club. Not even a trillion. And the only property they have is the best--a place teeming with life that would be impossible only a quarter of the planet's thickness above or below. A few of them build edifices reaching scant storeys into the sky; a few dig into the earth; there are so few of these that *not* being within a minute's travel from *literally* touching the planet's surface is exotic. But the unities, along with the rest of the planet's life, live in a tiny, priceless film adorned with the best resources they could ever know of."

Ployon was stunned. It thought of the cores of planets and asteroids it had been in. It thought of the ships and stations in space. Once it had had the privelege of working from a subnet hosted within a comparatively short distance of a planet's surface--it was a rare privilege, acquired through deft political maneuvering, and there were fewer than 130,982,539,813,209 other minds who had shared that privelege. And, basking in that luxury, it could only envy the minds which had bodies that walked on the surface. Ployon was stunned and reeling at the privilege of--

Ployon said, "How often do they travel to other planets?"

"There is only one planet so rich as to have them."

Ployon pondered the implications. It had travelled to half the spectrum of luxurious paradises. Had it been to even one this significant? Ployon reluctantly concluded that it had not. And that was not even considering what it meant for this golden plating to teem with life. And then Ployon realized that *each* of the unities had a *body* on that surface. It reeled in awe.

Archon said, "And you're not thinking about what it means that surface is home to the biological network, are you?"

Ployon was silent.

Archon said, "This organic biological network, in which they live and move and have their being--"

"Is God the organic?"

"Most of the things that the organic has, that are not to be found in our world, are reflections of God. But God is more. It is true that in God that they live and move and have their being, but it is truer. There is a significant minority that identifies the organic with God--"

Ployon interrupted, "--who are wrong--"

Archon interrupted, "--who are reacting against the destruction of the organic and seek the right thing in the wrong place--"

Ployon interrupted, "But how is God different from the organic?"

Archon sifted through a myriad of possible answers. "Hmm, this might be a good time for you to talk with that other mind you wanted to talk with."

"You know, you're good at piquing my curiosity."

"If you're looking for where they diverge, they don't. Or at least, some people would say they don't. Others who are deeply connected with God would say that the organic as we have been describing it is problematic--"

"But all unities are deeply connected with God, and disagreement is--"

"You're right, but that isn't where I was driving. And this relates to something messy, about disagreements when--"

"Aren't all unities able to calculate the truth from base axioms? Why would they disagree?"

Archon paused. "There are a myriad of real, not virtual disagreements--"

Ployon interrupted, "And it is part of a deeper reality to that world that--"

Archon interrupted. "No, no, or at best indirectly. There is something fractured about that world that--"

Ployon interrupted. "--is part of a tragic beauty, yes. Each thing that is artificially constricted in that world makes it greater. I'm waiting for the explanation."

"No. This does not make it greater."

"Then I'm waiting for the explanation of why this one limitation does *not* make it greater. But back to what you said about the real and the organic--"

"The differences between God and the organic are not differences of opposite directions. You are looking in the wrong place if you are looking for contradictions. It's more a difference like... if you knew what 'father' and 'mother' meant, male parent and female parent--"

Ployon interrupted, "--you know I have perfect details of male and female reproductive biology--"

Archon interrupted, "--and you think that if you knew the formula for something called chicken soup, you would know what the taste of chicken soup is for them--"

Ployon continued, "--so now you're going to develop some intricate elaboration of what it means that there is only one possible 'mother's' contribution, while outside of a laboratory the 'father's' contribution is extraordinarily haphazard..."

Archon said, "A complete non sequitur. If you only understand reproductive biology, you do not understand what a father or mother is. Seeing as how we have no concept yet of father or mother, let us look at something that's different enough but aligns with father/mother in an interesting enough way that... never mind."

Archon continued, "Imagine on the one hand a virtual reality, and on the other hand the creator of that virtual reality. You don't have to choose between moving in the virtual reality and being the creator's guest; the way to be the creator's guest is to move in the virtual reality and the purpose of moving in the virtual reality is being the creator's guest. But that doesn't mean that the creator is the virtual reality, or the virtual reality is the creator. It's not just a philosophical error to confuse them, or else it's a philosophical error with ramifications well outside of philosophy."

"Why didn't you just say that the relationship between God and the organic is creator/creation? Or that the organic is the world that was created?"

"Because the relationship is not that, or at very least not just that. And the organic is not the world--that is a philosophical error almost as serious as saying that the creator is the virtual reality, if a very different error. I fear that I have given you a simplification that is all the more untrue because of how true it is. God is in the organic, and in the world, and in each person, but not in the same way. How can I put it? If I say, 'God is in the organic,', it would be truer to say, 'The organic is not devoid of God,' because that is more ambiguous. If there were three boxes, and one contained a functional robot 'brain', and another contained a functional robot arm, and the third contained a non-functioning robot, it would be truer to say that each box contains something like a functioning robot than to say that each box contains a functioning robot. The ambiguity allows for being true in different ways in the different contexts, let alone something that words could not express even if we were discussing only one 'is in' or 'box'."

"Is there another way of expressing how their words would express it?"

"Their words are almost as weak as our words here."

"So they don't know about something this important?"

"Knowledge itself is different for them. To know something for us is to be able to analyze in a philosophical discussion. And this knowledge exists for them. But there is another root type of knowledge, a knowledge that--"

"Could you analyze the differences between the knowledge we use and the knowledge they use?"

"Yes, and it would be as useful to you as discussing biology. This knowledge is not entirely alien to us; when a mathematician 'soaks' in a problem, or I refused to connect with anything but the body, for a moment a chasm was crossed. But in that world the chasm doesn't exist... wait, that's too strong... a part of the chasm doesn't exist. Knowing is not with the mind alone, but the whole person--"

"What part of the knowing is stored in the bones?"

"Thank you for your flippancy, but people use the metaphor of knowledge being in their bones, or drinking, for this knowing."

"This sounds more like a physical process and some hankey-pankey that has been dignified by being called knowing. It almost sounds as if they don't have minds."

"They don't."

"*What?*"

"They don't, at least not as we know them. The mathematical analogy I would use is that they... never mind, I don't want to use a mathematical analogy. The computational analogy I would use is that we are elements of a computer simulation, and every now and then we break into a robot that controls the computer, and do something that transcends what elements of the computer simulation "should" be able to do. But they don't transcend the simulation because they were never elements of the simulation in the first place--they are real bodies, or real unities. And what I've called 'mind' in them is more properly understood as 'spirit', which is now a meaningless word to you, but is part of them that meets God whether they are aware of it or not. Speaking philosophically is a difficult discipline that few of them can do--"

"They are starting to sound mentally feeble."

"Yes, if you keep looking at them as an impoverished version of our world. It is hard to speak philosophically as it is hard for you to emulate a clock and do nothing else--because they need to drop out of several dimensions of their being to do it properly, and they live in those dimensions so naturally that it is an unnatural constriction for most of them to talk as if that was the only dimension of their being. And here I've been talking disappointingly about knowledge, making it sound more abstract than our knowing, when in fact it is much less so, and probably left you with the puzzle of how they manage to bridge gaps between mind, spirit, and body... but the difficulty of the question lies in a false setup. They are *unities* which experience, interact with, know all of them as united. And the knowing is deep enough that they can speculate that there's no necessary link between their spirits and bodies, or minds and bodies, or what have you. And if I can't explain this, I can't explain something even more foundational, the fact that the greatest thing about God is not how inconceivably majestic he is, but how close."

"It sounds as if--wait, I think you've given me a basis for a decent analysis. Let me see if I can--"

"Stop there."

"Why?"

Archon said, "Let me tell you a little story.

Archon continued, "A philosopher, Berkeley, believed that the only real things are minds and ideas and experiences in those minds: hence a rock was equal to the sum of every mind's impression of it. You could say that a rock existed, but what that had to mean was that there were certain sense impressions and ideas in minds, including God's mind; it didn't mean that there was matter outside of minds."

"A lovely virtual metaphysics. I've simulated that metaphysics, and it's enjoyable for a time."

"Yes, but for Berkeley it meant something completely different. Berkeley was a bishop,"

"What's a bishop?"

"I can't explain all of that now, but part of a bishop is a leader who is responsible for a community that believes God became a man, and helping them to know God and be unities."

"How does that reconcile with that metaphysics?"

Archon said, "Ployon, stop interrupting. He believed that they were not only compatible, but the belief that God became a man could only be preserved by his metaphysics. And he believed he was defending 'common sense', how most unities thought about the world.

Archon continued, "And after he wrote his theories, another man, Samuel Johnson, kicked a rock and said, 'I refute Berkeley thus!'"

Ployon said, "Ha ha! That's the way to score!"

"But he didn't score. Johnson established only one thing--"

"--how to defend against Berkeley--"

"--that he didn't understand Berkeley."

"Yes, he did."

"No, he didn't."

"But he did."

"Ployon, only the crudest understanding of Berkeley's ideas could mean that one could refute them by kicking a rock. Berkeley didn't make his ideas public until he could account for the sight of someone kicking a rock, or the experience of kicking it yourself, just as well as if there were matter outside of minds."

"I know."

"So now that we've established that--"

Ployon interrupted. "I know that Berkeley's ideas could account for kicking a rock as well as anything else. But kicking a rock is still an excellent way to refute Berkeley. If what you've said about this world has any coherence at all."

"*What?*"

"Well, Berkeley's ideas are airtight, right?"

"Ployon, there is no way they could be disproven. Not by argument, not by action."

"So it is in principle impossible to force someone out of Berkeley's ideas by argument."

"Absolutely."

"But you're missing something. What is it you've been talking to me about?"

"A world where mind and matter interpenetrate, and the organic, and there are many dimensions to life--"

"And if you're just falling further into a trap to logically argue, wouldn't it do something fundamentally *unity*-like to step into another dimension?"

Archon was silent.

Ployon said, "I understand that it would demonstrate a profound misunderstanding in our world... but wouldn't it say something equally profound in that world?"

Archon was stunned.

Ployon was silent for a long time.

Then Ployon said, "When are you going to refute Berkeley?"

Since the dawn of time, those who have walked the earth have looked up into the starry sky and wondered. They have asked, "What is the universe, and who are we?" "What are the woods?" "Where did this all come from?" "Is there life after death?" "What is the meaning of our existence?" The march of time has brought civilization, and with that, science. And science allows us to answer these age-old human questions.

That, at least, is the account of it that people draw now. But the truth is much more interesting.

Science is an ingenious mechanism to test guesses about mechanisms and behavior of the universe, and it is phenomenally powerful in that arena. Science can try to explain how the Heavens move, but it isn't the sort of thing to explain why there are Heavens that move that way--science can also describe how the Heavens have moved and reached their present position, but not the "Why?" behind it. Science can describe how to make technology to make life more convenient, but not "What is the meaning of life?" Trying to ask science to answer "Why?" (or for that matter, "Who?" or any other truly interesting question besides "How?") is a bit like putting a book on a scale and asking the scale, "What does this book mean?" And there are indeed some people who will accept the scale's answer, 429.7425 grams, as the definitive answer to what the book means, and all the better because it is so *precise*.

But to say that much and then stop is to paint a deceptive picture. *Very* deceptive. Why?

Science at that point had progressed more than at any point in history, and its effects were being felt around the world. And science enjoyed both a profound prestige and a profound devotion. Many people did not know what "understanding nature" could mean besides "learning scientific descriptions of nature," which was a bit like not knowing what "understanding your best friend" could mean besides "learning the biochemical building blocks of your friend's body."

All this and more is true, yet this is not the most important truth. This was the Middle Age between ancient and human society and the technological, and in fact it was the early Middle Age. People were beginning to develop real technologies, the seeds of technology we would recognize, and could in primitive fashion jack into such a network as existed then. But all of this was embraced in a society that was ancient, ancient beyond measure. As you may have guessed, it is an error to misunderstand that society as an inexplicably crude version of real technological society. It is a fundamental error.

To really understand this society, you need to understand not its technology, but the sense in which it was ancient. I will call it 'medieval', but you must understand that the ancient element in that society outweighs anything we would recognize.

And even this is deceptive, not because a single detail is wrong, but because it is abstract. I will tell you about certain parts in an abstract fashion, but you must understand that in this world's thinking the concrete comes *before* the abstract. I will do my best to tell a story--not as they would tell one, because that would conceal as much as it would reveal, but taking their way of telling stories and adapting it so we can see what is going on.

For all of their best efforts to spoil it, all of them live on an exquisite garden in the thin film where the emptiness of space meets the barrier of rock--there is a nest, a cradle where they are held tightly, and even if some of those who are most trying to be scientific want to flee into the barren wastes of space and other planets hostile to their kind of life. And this garden itself has texture, an incredible spectrum of texture along its surface. Place is itself significant, and I cannot capture what this story would have been like had it been placed in Petaling Jaya in Malaysia, or Paris in France, or Cambridge in England. What are these? I don't know... I can say that Petaling Jaya, Paris, and Cambridge are cities, but that would leave you knowing as much as you knew 5 milliseconds before I told you. And Malaysia, France, and England are countries, and now you know little besides being able to guess that a country is somehow capable of containing a city. Which is barely more than you knew before; the fact is that there is something very different between Petaling Jaya, Paris, and Cambridge. They have different wildlife and different places with land and water, but that is not nearly so interesting as the difference in people. I could say that people learn different skills, if I wanted to be very awkward and uninformative, but... the best way of saying it is that in our world, because there is nothing keeping minds apart... In that world, people have been separate so they don't even speak the same language. They almost have separate worlds. There is something common to all medievals, beyond what technology may bring, and people in other cities could find deep bonds with this story, but... Oh, there are many more countries than those I listed, and these countries have so many cities that you could spend your whole life travelling between cities and never see all of them. No, our world doesn't have this wealth. Wealthy as it is, it doesn't come close.

Petaling Jaya is a place of warm rainstorms, torrents of water falling from the sky, a place where a little stream of unscented water flows by the road, even if such a beautiful "open sewer" is not appreciated. Petaling Jaya is a place where people are less aware of time than in Cambridge or Paris and yet a place where people understand time better, because of reasons that are subtle and hard to understand. It draws people from three worlds in the grandeur that is Asia, and each of them brings treasures. The Chinese bring with them the practice of calling adults "Uncle" or "Aunt", my father's brother or my father's sister or my mother's brother or my mother's sister, which is to say, addresses them not only by saying that there is something great about them, but they are "tied by blood"--a bond that I do not know how to explain, save to say that ancestry and origins are not the mechanism of how they came to be, or at least not just the mechanism of how they came to be. Ancestry and origins tell of the substance of who they are, and that is one more depth that cannot exist in our world with matter and mind separate. The Indians and Bumi Putras--if it is really only them, which is far from true--live a life of friendship and hospitality, which are human treasures that shine in them. What is hospitality, you ask? That is hard to answer; it seems that anything I can say will be deceptive. It means that if you have a space, and if you allow someone in that space, you serve that person, caring for every of his needs. That is a strange virtue--and it will sound stranger when I say that this is not endured as inexpedient, but something where people want to call others. Is it an economic exchange? That is beside the point; these things are at once the shadow cast by real hospitality, and at the same time the substance of hospitality itself, and you need to understand men before you can understand it. What about friendship? Here I am truly at a loss. I can only say that in the story that I am about to tell, what happens is the highest form of friendship.

Paris is, or at least has been, a place with a liquid, a drug, that temporarily causes a pleasant mood while changing behavior and muddling a person's thoughts. But to say that misses what that liquid is, in Paris or much else. To some it is very destructive, and the drug is dangerous if it is handled improperly. But that is the hinge to something that--in our world, no pleasure is ever dangerous. You or I have experienced pleasures that these minds could scarcely dream of. We can have whatever pleasure we want at any time. And in a very real sense no pleasure *means* anything.

But in their world, with its weaker pleasures, every pleasure is connected to something. And this liquid, this pleasure, if taken too far, destroys people--which is a hinge, a doorway to something. It means that they need to learn a self-mastery in using this liquid, and in using it many of them forge a beauty in themselves that affects all of life. And they live beautiful lives. Beautiful in many ways. They are like Norsemen of ages past, who sided with the good powers, not because the good powers were going to win, but because they wanted to side with the good powers and fight alongside them when the good powers lost and chaos ruled. It is a tragic beauty, and the tragedy is all the more real because it is unneeded, but it is beauty, and it is a beauty that could not exist if they knew the strength of good. And I have not spoken of the beauty of the language in Paris, with its melody and song, or of the artwork and statues, the Basilica of the Sacré-Coeur, or indeed of the tapestry that makes up the city.

Cambridge is what many of them would call a "medieval" village, meaning that it has stonework that looks to its members like the ancient world's architecture. To them this is a major difference; the ancient character of the buildings to them overwhelms the fact that they are buildings. To that medieval world, both the newest buildings and the ones they considered "medieval" had doorways, stairwells, rooms, windows, and passages. You or I would be struck by the ancient character of the oldest and newest buildings and the ancient character of the life they serve. But to these medievals, the fact that a doorway was built out of machine-made materials instead of having long ago been shaped from stone takes the door--the *door*--from being ancient to being a new kind of thing! And so in the quaintest way the medievals consider Cambridge a "medieval" village, not because they were all medievals, but because the ancient dimension to *architecture* was more ancient to them than the equally ancient ways of constructing spaces that were reflected in the "new" buildings. There was more to it than that, but...

That was not the most interesting thing about them. I know you were going to criticize me for saying that hospitality was both a human treasure and something that contributed to the uniqueness of Petaling Jaya, but I need to do the same thing again. Politeness is... how can I describe it? Cynics describe politeness as being deceit, something where you learn a bunch of standard things to do and have to use them to hide the fact that you're offended, or bored, or want to leave, or don't like someone. And *all of that is true*--and deceptive. A conversation will politely begin with one person saying, "Hi, Barbara, how are you?" And Barbara will say, "Fine, George, how are you?" "Fine!" And the exact details seem almost arbitrary between cultures. This specific interaction is, on the surface, superficial and not necessarily true: people usually say they feel fine whether or not they really feel fine at all. And so politeness can be picked apart in this fashion, as if there's nothing else there, but *there is*. Saying "How are you?" opens a door, a door of concern. In one sense, what is given is very small. But if a person says, "I feel rotten," the other person is likely to listen. Barbara might only "give" George a little bit of chatter, but if he were upset, she would comfort him; if he were physically injured, she would call an ambulance to give him medical help; if he were hungry, she might buy him something to eat. But he only wants a little chat, so she only gives him a little chat--which is not really a little thing at all, but I'm going to pretend that it's small. Politeness stems from a concern for others, and is in actuality quite deep. The superficial "Hi, how are you?" is really not superficial at all. It is connected to a much deeper concern, and the exterior of rules is connected to a heart of concern. And Cambridge, which is a place of learning, and has buildings more ancient than what these medieval people usually see, is perhaps most significantly distinguished by its politeness.

But I have not been telling you a story. These observations may not be completely worthless, but they are still not a dynamic story. The story I'm about to tell you is not in Petaling Jaya, nor in Paris, nor in Cambridge, nor in any of thousands of other worlds. And I would like to show you what the medieval society looks like in action. And so let's look at Peter.

Peter, after a long and arduous trek, opened the car door, got out, stretched, looked at the vast building before him, and listened as his father said, "We've done it! The rest should be easy, at least for today." Then Peter smiled, and smashed his right thumb in the car door.

Then suddenly they moved--their new plan was to get to a hospital. Not much later, Peter was in the Central DuPage Hospital emergency room, watching people who came in after him be treated before him--not because they had more clout, but because they had worse injuries. The building was immense--something like one of our biological engineering centers, but instead of engineering bodies according to a mind's specification, this used science to restore bodies that had been injured and harmed, and reduce people's suffering. And it was incredibly primitive; at its best, it helped the bodies heal itself. But you must understand that even if these people were far wealthier than most others in their tiny garden, they had scant resources by our standard, and they made a major priority to restore people whose bodies had problems. (If you think about it, this tells something about how they view the value of each body.) Peter was a strong and healthy young man, and it had been a while since he'd been in a hospital. He was polite to the people who were helping him, even though he wished he were anywhere else.

You're wondering why he deliberately smashed his thumb? Peter didn't deliberately smash his thumb. He was paying attention to several other things and shoved the door close while his thumb was in its path. His body is not simply a device controlled by his mind; they interact, and his mind can't do anything he wishes it to do--he can't add power to it. He thinks by working with a mind that operates with real limitations and can overlook something in excitement--much like his body. If he achieves something, he doesn't just requisition additional mental power. He struggles within the capabilities of his own mind, and that means that when he achieves something with his mind, he *achieves* something. Yes, in a way that you or I cannot. Not only is his body in a very real sense more real to him than any of the bodies you or I have jacked into and swapped around, but his *mind* is more real. I'm not sure how to explain it.

Peter arrived for the second time well after check-in time, praying to be able to get in. After a few calls with a network that let him connect with other minds while keeping his body intact, a security officer came in, expressed sympathy about his bandaged thumb--what does 'sympathy' mean? It means that you share in another person's pain and make it less--and let him up to his room. The family moved his possessions from the car to his room and made his bed in a few minutes, and by the time it was down, the security guard had called the RA, who brought Peter his keys.

It was the wee hours of the morning when Peter looked at his new home for the second time, and tough as Peter was, the pain in his thumb kept the weary man from falling asleep. He was in as much pain as he'd been in for a while. What? Which part do you want explained? Pain is when the mind is troubled because the body is injured; it is a warning that the body needs to be taken care of. No, he can't turn it off just because he thinks it's served his purpose; again, you're not understanding the intimate link between mind and body. And the other thing... sleep is... Their small globe orbits a little star, and it spins as it turns. At any time, part of the planet faces the star, the sun, and part faces away, and on the globe, it is as if a moving wall comes, and all is light, then another wall comes, and it is dark. The globe has a rhythm of light and dark, a rhythm of day and night, and people live in intimate attunement to this rhythm. The ancients moved about when it was light and slept when it was dark--to sleep, at its better moments, is to come fatigued and have body and mind rejuvenate themselves to awaken full of energy. The wealthier medievals have the ability to see by mechanical light, to awaken when they want and fall asleep when they want--and yet they are still attuned, profoundly attuned, to this natural cycle and all that goes with it. For that matter, Peter can stick a substance into his body that will push away the pain--and yet, for all these artificial escapes, medievals feel pain and usually take care of their bodies by heeding it, and medievals wake more or less when it is light and sleep more or less when it is dark. And they don't think of pain as attunement to their bodies--most of them wish they couldn't feel pain, and certainly don't think of pain as good--nor do more than a few of them think in terms of waking and sleeping to a natural rhythm... but so much of the primeval way of being human is so difficult to dislodge for the medievals.

He awoke when the light was ebbing, and after some preparations set out, wandering this way and that until he found a place to eat. The pain was much duller, and he made his way to a selection of different foods--meant not only to nourish but provide a pleasant taste--and sat down at a table. There were many people about; he would not eat in a cell by himself, but at a table with others in a great hall.

A young man said, "Hi, I'm John." Peter began to extend his hand, then looked at his white bandaged thumb and said, "Excuse me for not shaking your hand. I am Peter."

A young woman said, "I'm Mary. I saw you earlier and was hoping to see you more."

Peter wondered about something, then said, "I'll drink for that," reached with his right hand, grabbed a glass vessel full of carbonated water with sugar, caffeine, and assorted unnatural ingredients, and then winced in pain, spilling the fluid on the table.

Everybody at the table moved. A couple of people dodged the flow of liquid; others stopped what they were doing, rushing to take earth toned objects made from the bodies of living trees (napkins), which absorbed the liquid and were then shipped to be preserved with other unwanted items. Peter said, "I keep forgetting I need to be careful about my thumb," smiled, grabbed another glass with fluid cows had labored to create, until his wet left hand slipped and he spilled the organic fluid all over his food.

Peter stopped, sat back, and then laughed for a while. "This is an interesting beginning to my college education."

Mary said, "I noticed you managed to smash your thumb in a car door without saying any words you regret. What else has happened?"

Peter said, "Nothing great; I had to go to the ER, where I

had to wait, before they could do something about my throbbing thumb. I got back at 4:00 AM and couldn't get to sleep for a long time because I was in so much pain. Then I overslept my alarm and woke up naturally in time for dinner. How about you?"

Mary thought for a second about the people she met. Peter could see the sympathy on her face.

John said, "Wow. That's nasty."

Peter said, "I wish we couldn't feel pain. Have you thought about how nice it would be to live without pain?"

Mary said, "I'd like that."

John said, "Um..."

Mary said, "What?"

John said, "Actually, there are people who don't feel pain, and there's a name for the condition. You've heard of it."

Peter said, "I haven't heard of that before."

John said, "Yes you have. It's called leprosy."

Peter said, "What do you mean by 'leprosy'? I thought leprosy was a disease that ravaged the body."

John said, "It is. But that is only because it destroys the ability to feel pain. The way it works is very simple. We all get little nicks and scratches, and because they hurt, we show extra sensitivity. Our feet start to hurt after a long walk, so without even thinking about it we... shift things a little, and keep anything really bad from happening. That pain you are feeling is your body's way of asking room to heal so that the smashed thumbnail (or whatever it is) that hurts so terribly now won't leave you permanently maimed. Back to feet, a leprosy patient will walk exactly the same way and get wounds we'd never even think of for taking a long walk. All the terrible injuries that make leprosy a feared disease happen *only* because leprosy keeps people from feeling pain."

Peter looked at his thumb, and his stomach growled.

John said, "I'm full. Let me get a drink for you, and then I'll help you drink it."

Mary said, "And I'll get you some dry food. We've already eaten; it must--"

Peter said, "Please, I've survived much worse. It's just a bit of pain."

John picked up a clump of wet napkins and threatened to throw it at Peter before standing up and walking to get something to drink. Mary followed him.

Peter sat back and just laughed.

John said, "We have some time free after dinner; let's just wander around campus."

They left the glass roofed building and began walking around. There were vast open spaces between buildings. They went first to "Blanchard", a building they described as "looking like a castle." Blanchard, a tall ivory colored edifice, built of rough limestone, which overlooked a large expanse adorned with a carefully tended and *living* carpet, had been modelled after a building in a much older institution called Oxford, and... this is probably the time to explain certain things about this kind of organization.

You and I simply requisition skills. If I were to imagine what it would mean to educate those people--or at least give skills; the concept of 'education' is slightly different from either inserting skills or inserting knowledge into a mind, and I don't have the ability to explain exactly what the distinction is here, but I will say that it is significant--then the obvious way is to simply make a virtual place on the network where people can be exposed to knowledge. And that model would become phenomenally popular within a few years; people would pursue an education that was a niche on such a network as they had, and would be achieved by weaving in these computer activities with the rest of their lives.

But this place preserved an ancient model of education, where disciples would come to live in a single place, which was in a very real sense its own universe, and meet in ancient, face-to-face community with their mentors and be shaped in more than what they know and can do. Like so many other things, it was ancient, using computers here and there and even teaching people the way of computers while avoiding what we would assume comes with computers.

But these people liked that building, as contrasted to buildings that seemed more modern, because it seemed to convey an illusion of being in another time, and let you forget that you were in a modern era.

After some wandering, Peter and those he had just met looked at the building, each secretly pretending to be in a more ancient era, and went through an expanse with a fountain in the center, listened to some music, and ignored clouds, trees, clusters of people who were sharing stories, listening, thinking, joking, and missing home, in order to come to something exotic, namely a rotating platform with a mockup of a giant mastodon which had died before the end of the last ice age, and whose bones had been unearthed in a nearby excavation. Happy to have seen something exotic, they ignored buildings which have a human-pleasing temperature the year round, other people excited to have seen new friends, toys which sailed through the air on the same principles as an airplane's wings, a place where artistic pieces were being drawn into being, a vast, stonehard pavement to walk, and a spectrum of artefacts for the weaving of music.

Their slow walk was interrupted when John looked at a number on a small machine he had attached to his wrist, and interpreted it to mean that it was time for the three of them to stop their leisured enjoyment of the summer night and move with discomfort and haste to one specific building--they all were supposed to go to the building called Fischer. After moving over and shifting emotionally from being relaxed and joyful to being bothered and stressed, they found that they were all on a brother and sister floor, and met their leaders.

Paul, now looking considerably more coherent than when he procured Peter's keys, announced, "Now, for the next exercise, I'll be passing out toothpicks. I want you to stand in two lines, guy-girl-guy-girl, and pass a lifesaver down the line. If your team passes the lifesaver to the end first, you win. Oh, and if you drop the lifesaver your team has to start over, so don't drop it."

People shuffled, and shortly Peter was standing in line,

looking over the shoulder of a girl he didn't know, and silently wishing he weren't playing this game. He heard a voice say, "Go!" and then had an intermittent view of a tiny sugary torus passing down the line and the two faces close to each other trying simultaneously to get close enough to pass the lifesaver, and control the clumsy, five centimeter long toothpicks well enough to transfer the candy. Sooner than he expected the girl turned around, almost losing the lifesaver on her toothpick, and then began a miniature dance as they clumsily tried to synchronize the ends of their toothpicks. This took unpleasantly long, and Peter quickly banished a thought of "This is almost kissing! That can't be what's intended." Then he turned around, trying both to rush and not to rush at the same time, and repeated the same dance with the young woman standing behind him--Mary! It was only after she turned away that Peter realized her skin had changed from its alabaster tone to pale rose.

Their team won, and there was a short break as the next game was organized. Peter heard bits of conversation: "This has been a bummer; I've gotten two papercuts this week." "--and then I--" "What instruments do you--" "I'm from France too! *Tu viens de Paris?*" "Really? You--" Everybody seemed to be chattering, and Peter wished he could be in one of--actually, several of those conversations at once.

Paul's voice cut in and said, "For this next activity we are going to form a human circle. With your team, stand in a circle, and everybody reach in and grab another hand with each hand. Then hold on tight; when I say, "Go," you want to untangle yourselves, without letting go. The first team to untangle themselves wins!"

Peter reached in, and found each of his hands clasped in a solid, masculine grip. Then the race began, and people jostled and tried to untangle themselves. This was a laborious process and, one by one, every other group freed itself, while Peter's group seemed stuck on--someone called and said, "I think we're knotted!" As people began to thin out, Paul looked with astonishment and saw that they were indeed knotted. "A special prize to them, too, for managing the best tangle!"

"And now, we'll have a three-legged race! Gather into pairs, and each two of you take a burlap sack. Then--" Paul continued, and with every game, the talk seemed to flow more. When the finale finished, Peter found himself again with John and Mary and heard the conversations flowing around him: "Really? You too?" "But you don't understand. Hicks have a slower pace of life; we enjoy things without all the things you city dwellers need for entertainment. And we learn resourceful ways to--" "--and only at Wheaton would the administration *forbid* dancing while *requiring* the games we just played and--" Then Peter lost himself in a conversation that continued long into the night. He expected to be up at night thinking about all the beloved people he left at home, but Peter was too busy thinking about John's and Mary's stories.

The next day Peter woke up when his machine played a hideous sound, and groggily trudged to the dining hall to eat some chemically modified grains and drink water that had been infused with traditionally roasted beans. There were pills he could have taken that would have had the effect he was looking for, but he savored the beverage, and after sitting at a table without talking, bounced around from beautiful building to beautiful building, seeing sights for the first time, and wishing he could avoid all that to just get to his advisor.

Peter found the appropriate hallway, wandered around nervously until he found a door with a yellowed plaque that said "Julian Johnson," knocked once, and pushed the door open. A white-haired man said, "Peter Jones? How are you? Do come in... What can I do for you?"

Peter pulled out a sheet of paper, an organic surface used to retain colored trails and thus keep small amounts of information inscribed so that the "real" information is encoded in a personal way. No, they don't need to be trained to have their own watermark in this encoding.

Peter looked down at the paper for a moment and said, "I'm sorry I'm late. I need you to write what courses I should take and sign here. Then I can be out of your way."

The old man sat back, drew a deep breath, and relaxed into a fatherly smile. Peter began to wonder if his advisor was going to say anything at all. Then Prof. Johnson motioned towards an armchair, as rich and luxurious as his own, and then looked as if he remembered something and offered a bowl full of candy. "Sit down, sit down, and make yourself comfortable. May I interest you in candy?" He picked up an engraved metal bowl and held it out while Peter grabbed a few Lifesavers.

Prof. Johnson sat back, silent for a moment, and said, "I'm sorry I'm out of butterscotch; that always seems to disappear. Please sit down, and tell me about yourself. We can get to that form in a minute. One of the priveleges of this job is that I get to meet interesting people. Now, where are you from?"

Peter said, "I'm afraid there's not much that's interesting about me. I'm from a small town downstate that doesn't have anything to distinguish itself. My amusements have been reading, watching the cycle of the year, oh, and running. Not much interesting in that. Now which classes should I take?"

Prof. Johnson sat back and smiled, and Peter became a little less tense. "You run?"

Peter said, "Yes; I was hoping to run on the track this afternoon, after the lecture. I've always wanted to run on a real track."

The old man said, "You know, I used to run myself, before I became an official Old Geezer and my orthopaedist told me my knees couldn't take it. So I have to content myself with swimming now, which I've grown to love. Do you know about the Prairie Path?"

Peter said, "No, what's that?"

Prof. Johnson said, "Years ago, when I ran, I ran through the areas surrounding the College--there are a lot of beautiful houses. And, just south of the train tracks with the train you can hear now, there's a path before you even hit the street. You can run, or bike, or walk, on a path covered with fine white gravel, with trees and prairie plants on either side. It's a lovely view." He paused, and said, "Any ideas what you want to do after

Wheaton?"

Peter said, "No. I don't even know what I want to major in."

Prof. Johnson said, "A lot of students don't know what they want to do. Are you familiar with Career Services? They can help you get an idea of what kinds of things you like to do."

Peter looked at his watch and said, "It's chapel time."

Prof. Johnson said, "Relax. I can write you a note." Peter began to relax again, and Prof. Johnson continued, "Now you like to read. What do you like to read?"

Peter said, "Newspapers and magazines, and I read this really cool book called *Zen and the Art of Motorcycle Maintenance.* Oh, and I like the Bible."

Prof. Johnson said, "I do too. What do you like about it most?"

"I like the stories in the Old Testament."

"One general tip: here at Wheaton, we have different kinds of professors--"

Peter said, "Which ones are best?"

Prof. Johnson said, "Different professors are best for different students. Throughout your tenure at Wheaton, ask your friends and learn which professors have teaching styles that you learn well with and mesh well with. Consider taking other courses from a professor you like. Now we have a lot of courses which we think expose you to new things and stretch you--people come back and see that these courses are best. Do you like science?"

"I like it; I especially liked a physics lab."

Prof. Johnson took a small piece of paper from where it was attached to a stack with a strange adhesive that had "failed" as a solid adhesive, but provided a uniquely useful way to make paper that could be attached to a surface with a slight push and then be detached with a gentle pull, remarkably enough without damage to the paper or the surface. He began to think, and flip through a book, using a technology thousands of years old at its heart. "Have you had calculus?" Prof. Johnson restrained himself from launching into a discussion of the grand, Utopian vision for "calculus" as it was first imagined and how different a conception it had from anything that would be considered "mathematics" today. Or should he go into that? He wavered, and then realized Peter had answered his question. "Ok," Prof. Johnson said, "the lab physics class unfortunately requires that you've had calculus. Would you like to take calculus now? Have you had geometry, algebra, and trigonometry?"

Peter said, "Yes, I did, but I'd like a little break from that now. Maybe I could take calculus next semester."

"Fair enough. You said you liked to read."

"Magazines and newspapers."

"Those things deal with the unfolding human story. I wonder if you'd like to take world civilization now, or a political science course."

"History, but why study world history? Why can't I just study U.S. history?"

Prof. Johnson said, "The story of our country is intertwined with that of our world. I think you might find that some of the things in world history are a lot closer to home than you think--and we have some real storytellers in our history department."

"That sounds interesting. What else?"

"The Theology of Culture class is one many students find enjoyable, and it helps build a foundation for Old and New Testament courses. Would you be interested in taking it for A quad or B quad, the first or second half of the semester?"

"Could I do both?"

"I wish I could say yes, but this course only lasts half the semester. The other half you could take Foundations of Wellness--you could do running as homework!"

"I think I'll do that first, and then Theology of Culture. That should be new," Peter said, oblivious to how tightly connected he was to theology and culture. "What else?"

Prof. Johnson said, "We have classes where people read things that a lot of people have found really interesting. Well, that could describe several classes, but I was thinking about Classics of Western Literature or Literature of the Modern World."

Peter said, "Um... Does Classics of Western Literature cover ancient and medieval literature, and Literature of the Modern World cover literature that isn't Western? Because if they do, I'm not sure I could connect with it."

Prof. Johnson relaxed into his seat, a movable support that met the contours of his body. Violating convention somewhat, he had a chair for Peter that was as pleasant to rest in as his own. "You know, a lot of people think that. But you know what?"

Peter said, "What?"

"There is something human that crosses cultures. That is why the stories have been selected. Stories written long ago, and stories written far away, can have a lot to connect with."

"Ok. How many more courses should I take?"

"You're at 11 credits now; you probably want 15. Now you said that you like *Zen and the Art of Motorcycle Maintenance*. I'm wondering if you would also like a philosophy course."

Peter said, "*Zen and the Art of Motorcycle Maintenance* is... I don't suppose there are any classes that use that. Or are there? I've heard Pirsig isn't given his fair due by philosophers."

Prof. Johnson said, "If you approach one of our philosophy courses the way you approach *Zen and the Art of Motorcycle Maintenance*, I think you'll profit from the encounter. I wonder if our Issues and Worldviews in Philosophy might interest you. I'm a big fan of thinking worldviewishly, and our philosophers have some pretty interesting things to say."

Peter asked, "What does 'worldviewishly' mean?"

Prof. Johnson said, "It means thinking in terms of worldviews. A worldview is the basic philosophical framework that gives shape to how we view the world. Our philosophers will be able to help you understand the basic issues surrounding worldviews and craft your own Christian worldview. You may find this frees you from the Enlightenment's secularizing influence--and if you don't know what the Enlightenment is now, you will learn to understand it, and its problems, and how you can be free of them." He spoke with the same simplistic assurance of artificial intelligence researchers who, seeing the power of computers and recognizing how simple certain cognitive feats are for humans, assumed that it was only a matter of time that artificial intelligence would "bridge the gap"--failing to recognize the tar pit of the peaks of intelligence that seem so deceptively simple and easy to human phenomenology. For computers could often defeat the best human players at chess--as computerlike a human skill as one might reasonably find--but deciphering the language of a children's book or walking through an unfamiliar room, so easy to humans, seemed more difficult for computers the more advanced research began. Some researchers believed that the artificial intelligence project had uncovered the non-obvious significance of a plethora of things humans take for granted--but the majority still believed that what seemed trivial for humans must be the sort of thinking a computer can do, because there is no other kind of thinking... and an isomorphic simplicity, an apparent and deceptive simplicity much like this one, made it seem as if ideas were all that really mattered: not all that existed, but all that had an important influence. Prof. Johnson did not consciously understand how the Enlightenment worldview--or, more accurately, the Enlightenment--created the possibility of seeing worldviews that way, nor did he see how strange the idea of crafting one's own worldview would seem to pre-Enlightenment Christians. He did not realize that his own kindness towards Peter was not simply because he agreed with certain beliefs, but because of a deep and many-faceted way in which he had walked for decades, and walked well. It was with perfect simplicity that he took this way for granted, as artificial intelligence researchers took for granted all the things which humans did so well they seemed to come naturally, and framed worldviewish thought as carrying with it everything he assumed from his way.

Peter said, "Ok. Well, I'll take those classes. It was good to meet you."

Prof. Johnson looked over a document that was the writeup of a sort of game, in which one had a number of different rooms that were of certain sizes, and certain classes had requirements about what kind of room they needed for how long, and the solution involved not only solving the mathematical puzzle, but meeting with teachers and caring for their concerns, longstanding patterns, and a variety of human dimensions derisively labelled as "political." Prof. Johnson held in his hands the schedule with the official solution for that problem, and guided Peter to an allowable choice of class sections, taking several different actions that were considered "boring paperwork."

Prof. Johnson said, "I enjoyed talking with you. Please do take some more candy--put a handful in your pocket or something. I just want to make one more closing comment. I want to see you succeed. Wheaton wants to see you succeed. There are some rough points and problems along the way, and if you bring them to me I can work with them and try to help you. If you want to talk with your RA or our chaplain or someone else, that's fine, but please... my door is *always* open. And it was good to meet you too! Goodbye!"

Peter walked out, completely relaxed.

The next activity, besides nourishing himself with lunch (and eating, sleeping, and many other activities form a gentle background rhythm to the activities people are more conscious of. I will not describe each time Peter eats and sleeps, even though the 100th time in the story he eats with his new friends is as significant as the first, because I will be trying to help you see it their way), requires some explanation.

The term "quest," to the people here, is associated with an image of knights in armor, and a body of literature from writers like Chretien de Troyes and Sir Thomas Mallory who described King Arthur and his knights. In Chretien de Troyes, the knight goes off in various adventures, often quests where he is attempting different physical feats. In Sir Thomas Mallory, a new understanding of quests is introduced, in the quest for the holy grail--a legendary treasure which I cannot here explain save to say that it profoundly altered the idea of a quest, and the quest took a large enough place in many people's consciousness that it is used as a metaphor of the almost unattainable object of an ultimate pursuit (so that physicists would say that a grand unified theory which crystallizes all physical laws into a few simple equations is the "holy grail of physics"), and that the holy grail is itself in the shadow of a greater treasure, and this treasure was one many people in fact had possessed (some after great struggle, while others had never known a time when they were without it). In Mallory in particular the quest can be more than a physical task; most of Arthur's knights could not reach the holy grail because of--they weren't physical blemishes and they weren't really mental blemishes either, but what they were is hard to say. The whole topic (knights, quests, the holy grail...) connects to something about that world that is beyond my ability to convey; suffice it to say that it is connected with one more dimension we don't have here.

Peter, along with another group of students, went out on a quest. The object of this quest was to acquire seven specific items, on conditions which I will explain below:

1. "A dog biscuit." In keeping with a deeply human trait, the food they prepare is not simply what they judge adequate to sustain the body, but meant to give pleasure, in a sense adorned, because eating is not to them simply a biological need. They would also get adorned food to give pleasure to organisms they kept, including dogs, which include many different breeds which in turn varied from being natural sentries protecting territories to a welcoming committee of one which would give a visitor an exuberant greeting just because he was there.
2. "An M16 rifle's spent shell casing." That means the used remnant after... wait a little bit. I need to go a lot farther back to explain this one.

   You will find something deceptively familiar in that in that universe, people strategically align resources and then attack their opponents, usually until a defeat is obvious. And if you look for what is deceptive, it will be a frustrating search, because even if the technologies involved are primitive, it is a match of strategy, tactics, and opposition.

What makes it different is that this is not a recreation or an art form, but something many of them consider the worst evil that can happen, or among the worst. The resources that are destroyed, the bodies--in our world, it is simply what is involved in the game, but many of them consider it an eternal loss.

Among the people we will be meeting, people may be broken down into "pacifists" who believe that war is always wrong, and people who instead of being pure pacifists try to have a practical way of pursuing pacifist goals: the disagreement is not whether one should have a war for amusement's sake (they both condemn that), but what one should do when not having a war looks even more destructive than having a war. And that does not do justice to either side of the debate, but what I want to emphasize that to both of them this is not simply a game or one form of recreation; it is something to avoid at almost *any* cost.

A knight was someone who engaged in combat, an elite soldier riding an animal called a horse. In Chretien de Troye's day and Mallory's day, the culture was such that winning a fight was important, but fighting according to "chivalry" was more important. Among other things, chivalry meant that they would only use simple weapons based on mechanical principles--no poison--and they wouldn't even use weapons with projectiles, like arrows and (armor piercing) crossbow bolts. In practice that only meant rigid piercing and cutting weapons, normally swords and spears. And there was a lot more. A knight was to protect women and children.

The form that chivalry took in Peter's day allowed projectile weapons, although poison was still not allowed, along with biological, thermonuclear, and other weapons which people did not wish to see in war, and the fight to disfigure the tradition's understanding women had accorded them meant that women could fight and be killed like men, although people worked to keep children out of warfare, and in any case the "Geneva Convention", as the code of chivalry was called, maintained a sharp distinction between combatants and non-combatants, the latter of which were to be protected.

The specific projectile weapon carried by most members of the local army was called an M16 rifle, which fired surprisingly small .22 bullets--I say "surprisingly" because if you were a person fighting against them and you were hit, you would be injured but quite probably not killed.

This was intentional. (Yes, they knew how to cause an immediate kill.)

Part of it is the smaller consideration that if you killed an enemy soldier immediately, you took one soldier out of action; on the other hand, if you wounded an enemy soldier, you took three soldiers out of action. But this isn't the whole reason. The much bigger part of the reason is that their sense of chivalry (if it was really just chivalry; they loved their enemies) meant that even in their assaults they tried to subdue with as little killing as possible.

There were people training with the army in that community (no, not Peter; Peter was a pure pacifist) who trained, with M16 rifles, not because they wanted to fight, but as part of a not entirely realistic belief that if they trained hard enough, their achievement would deter people who would go to war. And the "Crusader battalion" (the Crusaders were a series of people who fought to defend Peter's spiritual ancestors from an encroaching threat that would have destroyed them) had a great sense of chivalry, even if none of them used the word "chivalry".

3. "A car bumper." A car bumper is a piece of armor placed on the front and back of cars so that they can sustain low-velocity collisions without damage. (At higher velocities, newer cars are designed to serve as a buffer so that "crumple zones" will be crushed, absorbing enough of the impact so that the "passenger cage" reduces injuries sustained by people inside; this is part of a broader cultural bent towards minimizing preventable death because of what they believe about one human life.) Not only is a car bumper an unusual item to give, it is heavy and awkward enough that people tend not to carry such things with them--even the wealthy ones tend to be extraordinarily lightly encumbered.
4. "An antique." It is said, "The problem with England is that they believe 100 miles is a long distance, and the problem with America is that they believe 100 years is a long time." An antique--giving the rule without all the special cases and exceptions, which is to say giving the rule as if it were not human--is something over 100 years old. To understand this, you must appreciate that it does not include easily available rocks, many of which are millions or billions of years old, and it is not based on the elementary particles that compose something (one would have to search hard to find something *not* made out of elementary particles almost as old as the universe). The term "antique" connotes rarity, and in a sense something out of the ordinary; that people's

way is concerned with "New! New! New!" and it is hard to find an artifact that was created more than 100 years ago, which is what was intended.

This quest is all the more interesting because there is an "unwritten rule" that items will be acquired by asking, not by theft or even purchase--and, as most antiques are valuable, it would be odd for someone you've just met--and therefore with whom you have only the general human bond but not the special bond of friendship--to give you such an item, even if most of the littler things in life are acquired economically while the larger things can only be acquired by asking.

5. "A note from a doctor, certifying that you do not have bubonic plague." Intended as a joke, this refers to a health, safeguarded by their medicine, which keeps them from a dreadful disease which tore apart societies some centuries ago: that sort of thing wasn't considered a live threat because of how successful their medicine was (which is why it could be considered humorous).
6. "A burning piece of paper which no one in your group lit. (Must be presented in front of Fischer and not brought into the building.)" This presents a physical challenge, in that there is no obvious way to transport a burning piece of paper--or what people characteristically envision as a burning piece of paper--from almost anywhere else to in front of Fischer.
7. "A sheet of paper with a fingerpaint handprint from a kindergartener."

   "Kindergarten" was the first year of their formal education, and a year of preparation before students were ready to enter their first grade. What did this society teach at its first, required year? Did it teach extraordinarily abstract equations, or cosmological theory, or literary archetypes, or how to use a lathe?

All of these could be taught later on, and for that matter there is reason to value all of them. But the very beginning held something different. It taught people to take their turn and share; it taught people "Do unto others as you would have them do unto you," the Golden Rule by which their great Teachers crystallized so much wisdom. All of this work and play, some of the most advanced lessons they could learn, were placed, not at the end, but at the *beginning* of their education.

That is what kindergarten was. What was a kindergartener? The true but uninformative answer would be "a person in kindergarten."

To get past that uninformative answer, I need to stress that their minds are bound up with organic life--they did *not* spring, fully formed, as you and I did. In most complex organisms, there is a process that transforms a genetically complete organism of just one cell to become a mature member of the species; among humans, that process is one of the longest and most complex. During that time their minds are developping as well as their bodies; in that regard they are not simply in harmony with the natural world this society believes it is separate from... but one of its best examples.

But to say that alone is to flatten out something interesting... even more interesting than the process of biological mental development is the place that society has for something called "childhood". Not all cultures have that concept--and again I am saying "culture" without explaining what it means. I can't. Not all societies understand "childhood" as this

> society does; to many, a child is a smaller and less capable adult, or even worse, a nonentity. But in this culture, childhood is a distinctive time, and a child, including a kindergardener, is something special--almost a different species of mind. Their inability to healthily sustain themselves is met, not always with scorn, but with a giving of support and protection--and this is not always a grudging duty, but something that can bring joy. They are viewed as innocent, which is certainly not true, and something keeps many people from resenting them when they prove that they are not innocent by doing things that would not be tolerated if an adult did it. And the imperviousness of this belief to contrary experience is itself the shadow of the whole place of childhood as a time to play and learn and explore worlds of imagination and the things most adults take for granted. And many adults experience a special pleasure, and much more than a pleasure, from the company of children, a pleasure that is tied to something much deeper.
>
> This pleasure shines through even a handprint left with "fingerpaints," a way of doing art reserved for children, so that this physical object is itself a symbol of all that is special about childhood, and like symbols of that world carries with it what is evoked: seeing such a handprint is a little like seeing a kindergartener.

And they were off. They stopped for a brief break and annoyedly watched the spectacle of over a hundred linked metal carts carrying a vast quantity of material, and walked in and out of the surrounding neighborhoods. Their knocks on the door met a variety of warm replies. Before long, they had a handprint from a kindergartener, a dog biscuit (and some very enthusiastic attention from a kind dog!), a note from an off-duty doctor (who did not examine them, but simply said that if they had the bubonic plague there would be buboes bulging from them in an obvious way), a cigarette lighter and a sheet of paper (unlit), a twisted bumper (which Peter surprised people by flipping over his shoulder), and finally a spent shell casing from a military science professor. When they climbed up "Fischer beach," John handed the paper and lighter to his RA and said, "Would you light this?" It was with an exhausted satisfaction that they went to dinner and had entirely amiable conversation with other equally students who scant minutes ago had been their competitors.

When dinner was finished, Peter and Mary sat for a while in exhausted silence, before climbing up for the next scheduled activity--but I am at a loss for how to describe the next scheduled activity. To start with, I will give a deceptive description. If you can understand this activity, you will have understood a great deal more of what is in that world that doesn't fit in ours.

Do I have to give a deceptive description, in that any description in our terms will be more or less deceptive? I wasn't trying to make that kind of philosophical point; I wasn't tring to make a philosophical point at all. I am choosing a description of the next scheduled activity that is more deceptive than it needs to be.

When students studied an academic discipline called "physics," the curriculum was an initiation into progressively stranger and more esoteric doctrines, presented at the level which students were able to receive them. Students were first taught "Newtonian mechanics" (which openly regarded as false), before being initiated into "Einstein's relativity" at the next level (which was also considered false, but was widely believed to be closer to the truth). Students experienced a "night and day" difference between Newtonian mechanics and all higher order mysteries. If you were mathematically adept enough to follow the mathematics, then Newton was easy because he agreed with good old common sense, and Einstein and even stranger mysteries were hard to understand because they turned common sense on its head. Newton was straightforward while the others were profoundly counterintuitive. So Einstein, unlike Newton, required a student to mentally engulf something quite alien to normal, common sense ways of thinking about the world around oneself. Hence one could find frustrated student remarks about, "And God said, 'Let there be light!' And there was Newton. Then the Devil howled, 'Let Einstein be!' and restored the status quo."

Under this way of experiencing physics, Newton simply added mathematical formality to what humans always knew: everything in space fit in one long and continuous three-dimensional grid, and time could be measured almost as if it were a line, and so Einstein was simply making things more difficult and further from humans' natural perceptions when his version of a fully mathematical model softened the boundaries of space and time so that one could no longer treat it as if it had a grid for a skeleton.

Someone acquainted with the history of science might make the observation that it was not so much that Newton's mechanics were a mathematically rigorous formalization of how people experienced space and time, but that how people experienced space and time had *become* a hazy and non-mathematical paraphrase of Newtonian mechanics: in other words, some students some students learned Newtonian mechanics easily, not because Newtonian physics was based on common sense, but because their "common sense" had been profoundly shaped by Newtonian physics.

This seemingly pedantic distinction was deeply tied to how the organic was being extinguished in their society.

I suspect you are thinking, "What other mathematical model was it based on instead?" And that's why you're having trouble guessing the answer.

The answer is related to the organic. Someone who knew Newton and his colleagues, and what they were rebelling against, could get a sense of something very different even without understanding what besides mathematics would undergird what space meant to them. In a certain sense, Newton forcefully stated the truth, but in a deceptive way. He worked hard to forge a concept of cold matter, pointing out that nature was not human--and it was a philosophical error to think of nature as human, but it was not nearly so great as one might think. Newton and his colleagues powerfully stressed that humans were superior to the rest of the physical world (which was not human), that they were meant not simply to be a part of nature but to conquer and rule it. And in so doing they attacked an equally great truth, that not only other life but even "inanimate" matter was kin to humans--lesser kin, perhaps, but humans and the rest of the natural world formed a continuity. They obscured the wisdom that the lordship humans were to exercise was not of a despot controlling something worthless, but the mastery of the crowning jewel of a treasure they had been entrusted to them. They introduced the concept of "raw material", something as foreign to their thinking as... I can't say what our equivalent would be, because everything surrounding "raw material" is so basic to us, and what they believed instead, their organic perception, is foreign to us. They caused people to forget that, while it would be a philosophical error to literally regard the world as human, it would be much graver to believe it is fundamentally described as inert, cold matter. And even when they had succeeded in profoundly influencing their cultures, so that people consciously believed in cold matter to a large degree, vestiges of the ancient experience survived in the medieval. It is perhaps not a coincidence that hundreds of years since Newton, in Newton's own "mother tongue" (English), the words for "matter" and "mother" both sprung from the same ancient root word.

The Newtonian conception of space had displaced to some degree the older conception of place, a conception which was less concerned with how far some place was from other different places, and more concerned with a sort of color or, to some extent, meaning. The older conception also had a place for some things which couldn't really be stated under the new conception: people would say, "You can't be in two places at once." What they meant by that was to a large degree something different, "Your body cannot be at two different spatial positions at the same time." This latter claim was deceptive, because it was true so far as it goes, but it was a very basic fact of life that people could be in two places at once. The entire point of the next scheduled activity was to be in two places at once.

Even without describing what the other place was (something which could barely be suggested even in that world) and acknowledging that the point of the activity was to be in two places at once, this description of that activity would surprise many of the people there, and disturb those who could best sense the other place. The next scheduled activity was something completely ordinary to them, a matter of fact event that held some mystery, and something that would not occur to them as being in two places at once. The activity of being present in two or more places at once was carried on, on a tacit level, even when people had learned to conflate place with mathematical position. One such activity was confused with what we do when we remember: when we remember, we recall data from storage, while they cause the past to be present. The words, "This do in rememberance of me," from a story that was ancient but preserved in the early medieval period we are looking at, had an unquestioned meaning of, "Cause me to be present by doing this," but had suffered under a quite different experience of memory, so that to some people it meant simply to go over data about a person who had been present in the past but could not be present then.

But this activity was not remembering. Or at least, it was not *just* remembering. And this leaves open the difficulty of explaining how it was ordinary to them. It was theoretically in complete continuity with the rest of their lives, although it would be more accurate to say that the rest of their lives were theoretically in complete continuity with it. This activity was in a sense the most human, and the most organic, in that in it they led the beasts of the field, the birds of the air, the fish of the sea, the plants, the rocks, the mountains, and the sees in returning to the place they came from. This description would also likely astonish the people who were gathered in a painted brick room, sitting on carpet and on movable perches, and seeing through natural light mixed with flickering fluorescent lights. Not one of them was thinking about "nature."

What went on there was in a very real sense mediocre. Each activity was broken down, vulgarized, compared to what it could be--which could not obliterate what was going on. When they were songs, they were what were called "7-11" songs, a pejorative term which meant songs with seven words repeated eleven times. There was a very real sense in which the event was diminished by the music, but even when you factor in every diminishing force, there was something going on there, something organic and more than organic, which you and I do not understand--for that matter, which many people in that world do not understand.

Archon was silent for a long time.

Ployon said, "What is it?"

Archon said, "I can't do it. I can't explain this world. All I've really been doing is taking the pieces of that world that are a bit like ours. You've been able to understand much of it because I haven't tried to convey several things that are larger than our world. 'God' is still a curious and exotic appendage that isn't connected to anything, not really; I haven't been able to explain, really explain, what it is to be male and female unities, or what masculinity and femininity are. There are a thousand things, and... I've been explaining what three-dimensional substance is to a two-dimensional world, and the way I've been doing it is to squash it into two dimensions, and make it understandable by removing from it everything that makes it three dimensional. Or almost everything..."

"How would a three dimensional being, a person from that world, explain the story?"

"But it wouldn't. A three dimensional being wouldn't collapse a cube into a square to make it easier for itself to understand; that's something someone who couldn't free itself from reading two dimensional thinking into three dimensions would do. You're stuck in two dimensions. So am I. That's why I failed, utterly failed, to explain the "brother-sister floor fellowship", the next scheduled activity. And my failure is structural. It's like I've been setting out to copy a living, moving organism by sculpturing something that looks like it out of steel. And what I've been doing is making intricate copies of its every contour, and painting the skin and fur exactly the same color, and foolishly hoping it will come alive. And this is something I can't make by genetic engineering."

"But how would someone from that world explain the story? Even if I can't understand it, I want to know."

"But people from that world don't explain stories. A story isn't something you *explain*; it's something that may be told, shared, but usually it is a social error to explain a story, because a story participates in human life and telling a story connects one human to another. And so it's a fundamental error to think a story is something you convey by explaining it--like engineering a robotic body for an animal so you can allow it to have a body. I have failed because I was trying something a mind could only fail at."

"Then can you tell the story, like someone from that world would tell it?"

Peter and Mary both loved to run, but for different reasons. Peter was training himself for various races; he had not joined track, as he did in high school, but there were other races. Mary ran to feel the sun and wind and rain. And, without any conscious effort, they found themselves running together down the prairie path together, and Peter clumsily learning to match his speed to hers. And, as time passed, they talked, and talked, and talked, and talked, and their runs grew longer.

When the fall break came, they both joined a group going to the northwoods of Wisconsin for a program that was half-work and half-play. And each one wrote a letter home about the other. Then Peter began his theology of culture class, and said, "This is what I want to study." Mary did not have a favorite class, at least not that she realized, until Peter asked her what her favorite class was and she said, "Literature."

When Christmas came, they went to their respective homes and spent the break thinking about each other, and they talked about this when they returned. They ended the conversation, or at least they thought they did, and then each hurried back to catch the other and say one more thing, and then the conversation turned out to last much longer, and ended with a kiss.

Valentine's Day was syrupy. It was trite enough that their more romantically inclined friends groaned, but it did not seem at all trite or syrupy to them. As Peter's last name was Patrick, he called Mary's father and prayed that St. Patrick's Day would be a momentous day for both of them.

Peter and Mary took a slow run to a nearby village, and had dinner at an Irish pub. Amidst the din, they had some hearty laughs. The waitress asked Mary, "Is there anything else that would make this night memorable?" Then Mary saw Peter on his knee, opening a jewelry box with a ring: "I love you, Mary. Will you marry me?"

Mary cried for a good five minutes before she could answer. And when she had answered, they sat in silence, a silence that overpowered the din. Then Mary wiped her eyes and they went outside.

It was cool outside, and the moon was shining brightly. Peter pulled a camera from his pocket, and said, "Stay where you are. Let me back up a bit. And hold your hand up. You look even more beautiful with that ring on your finger."

Peter's camera flashed as he took a picture, just as a drunk driver slammed into Mary. The sedan spun into a storefront, and Mary flew up into the air, landed, and broke a beer bottle with her face.

People began to come out, and in a few minutes the police and paramedics arrived. Peter somehow managed to answer the police officers' questions and to begin kicking himself for being too stunned to act.

When Peter left his room the next day, he looked for Prof. Johnson. Prof. Johnson asked, "May I give you a hug?" and then sat there, simply being with Peter in his pain. When Peter left, Prof. Johnson said, "I'm not just here for academics. I'm here for you." Peter went to chapel and his classes, feeling a burning rage that almost nothing could pierce. He kept going to the hospital, and watching Mary with casts on both legs and one arm, and many tiny stitches on her face, fluttering on the borders of consciousness. One time Prof. Johnson came to visit, and he said, "I can't finish my classes." Prof. Johnson looked at him and said, "The college will give you a full refund." Peter said, "Do you know of any way I can stay here to be with Mary?" Prof. Johnson said, "You can stay with me. And I believe a position with UPS would let you get some income, doing something physical. The position is open for you." Prof. Johnson didn't mention the calls he'd made, and Peter didn't think about them. He simply said, "Thank you."

A few days later, Mary began to be weakly conscious. Peter finally asked a nurse, "Why are there so many stitches on her face? Was she cut even more badly than--"

The nurse said, "There are a lot of stitches very close together because the emergency room had a cosmetic surgeon on duty. There will still be a permanent mark on her face, but some of the wound will heal without a scar."

Mary moved the left half of her mouth in half a smile. Peter said, "That was a kind of cute smile. How come she can smile like that?"

The nurse said, "One of the pieces of broken glass cut a nerve. It is unlikely she'll ever be able to move part of her face again."

Peter looked and touched Mary's hand. "I still think it's really quite cute."

Mary looked at him, and then passed out.

Peter spent a long couple of days training and attending to practical details. Then he came back to Mary.

Mary looked at Peter, and said, "It's a Monday. Don't you have classes now?"

Peter said, "No."

Mary said, "Why not?"

Peter said, "I want to be here with you."

Mary said, "I talked with one of the nurses, and she said

that you dropped out of school so you could be with me.

"Is that true?" she said.

Peter said, "I hadn't really thought about it that way."

Mary closed her eyes, and when Peter started to leave because he decided she wanted to be left alone, she said, "Stop. Come here."

Peter came to her bedside and knelt.

Mary said, "Take this ring off my finger."

Peter said, "Is it hurting you?"

Mary said, "No, and it is the greatest treasure I own. Take it off and take it back."

Peter looked at her, bewildered. "Do you not want to marry me?"

Mary said, "This may sting me less because I don't remember our engagement. I don't remember anything that happened near that time; I have only the stories others, even the nurses, tell me about a man who loves me very much."

Peter said, "But don't you love me?"

Mary forced back tears. "Yes, I love you, yes, I love you. And I know that you love me. You are young and strong, and have the love to make a happy marriage. You'll make some woman a very good husband. I thought that woman would be me.

"But I can see what you will not. You said I was beautiful, and I was. Do you know what my prognosis is? I will probably be able to stand. At least for short periods of time. If I'm fortunate, I may walk. With a walker. I will never be able to run again--Peter, I am nobody, and I have no future. Absolutely nobody. You are young and strong. Go and find a woman who is worth your love."

Mary and Peter both cried for a long time. Then Peter walked out, and paused in the doorway, crying. He felt torn inside, and then went in to say a couple of things to Mary. He said, "I believe in miracles."

Then Mary cried, and Peter said something else I'm not going to repeat. Mary said something. Then another conversation began.

The conversation ended with Mary saying, "You're stupid,

Peter. You're really, really stupid. I love you. I don't deserve such love. You're making a mistake. I love you." Then Peter went to kiss Mary, and as he bent down, he bent his mouth to meet the lips that he still saw as "really quite cute."

The stress did not stop. The physical therapists, after time, wondered that Mary had so much fight in her. But it stressed her, and Peter did his job without liking it. Mary and Peter quarreled and made up and quarreled and made up. Peter prayed for a miracle when they made up and sometimes when they quarreled. Were this not enough stress, there was an agonizingly long trial--and knowing that the drunk driver was behind bars surprisingly didn't make things better. But Mary very slowly learned to walk again. After six months, if Peter helped her, she could walk 100 yards before the pain became too great to continue.

Peter hadn't been noticing that the stress diminished, but he did become aware of something he couldn't put his finger on. After a night of struggling, he got up, went to church, and was floored by the Bible reading of, "You have heard that it was said, 'Love your neighbor and hate your enemy.' But I tell you, love your enemies and pray for those who persecute you." and the idea that when you do or do not visit someone in prison, you are visiting or refusing to visit Christ. Peter absently went home, tried to think about other things, made several phone calls, and then forced himself to drive to one and only one prison.

He stopped in the parking lot, almost threw up, and then steeled himself to go inside. He found a man, Jacob, and... Jacob didn't know who Peter was, but he recognized him as looking familiar. It was an awkward meeting. Then he recognized him as the man whose now wife he had crippled. When Peter left, he vomited and felt like a failure. He talked about it with Mary...

That was the beginning of a friendship. Peter chose to love the man in prison, even if there was no pleasure in it. And that created something deeper than pleasure, something Peter couldn't explain.

As Peter and Mary were planning the wedding, Mary said, "I want to enter with Peter next to me, no matter what the tradition says. It will be a miracle if I have the strength to stand for the whole wedding, and if I have to lean on someone I want it to be Peter. And I don't want to sit on a chair; I would rather spend my wedding night wracked by pain than go through my wedding supported by something lifeless!"

When the rehearsal came, Mary stood, and the others winced at the pain in her face. And she stood, and walked, for the entire rehearsal without touching Peter once. Then she said, "I can do it. I can go through the wedding on my own strength," and collapsed in pain.

At the wedding, she stood next to Peter, walking, her face so radiant with joy that some of the guests did not guess she was in exquisite pain. They walked next to each other, not touching, and Mary slowed down and stopped in the center of the church. Peter looked at her, wondering what Mary was doing.

Then Mary's arm shot around Peter's neck, and Peter stood startled for a moment before he placed his arm around her, squeezed her tightly, and they walked together to the altar.

On the honeymoon, Mary told Peter, "You are the only person I need." This was the greatest bliss either of them had known, and the honeymoon's glow shined and shined.

Peter and Mary agreed to move somewhere less expensive to settle down, and were too absorbed in their wedded bliss and each other to remember promises they had made earlier, promises to seek a church community for support and friends. And Peter continued working at an unglamorous job, and Mary continued fighting to walk and considered the housework she was capable of doing a badge of honor, and neither of them noticed that the words, "I love you" were spoken ever so slightly less frequently, nor did they the venom creeping into their words.

One night they exploded. What they fought about was not important. What was important was that Peter left, burning with rage. He drove, and drove, until he reached Wheaton, and at daybreak knocked on Prof. Johnson's door. There was anger in his voice when he asked, "Are you still my friend?"

Prof. Johnson got him something to eat and stayed with him

when he fumed with rage, and said, "I don't care if I'm supposed to be with her, I can't go back!" Then Prof. Johnson said, "Will you make an agreement with me? I promise you I won't ever tell you to go back to her, or accept her, or accept what she does, or apologize to her, or forgive her, or in any way be reconciled. But I need you to trust me that I love you and will help you decide what is best to do."

Peter said, "Yes."

Prof. Johnson said, "Then stay with me. You need some rest. Take the day to rest. There's food in the fridge, and I have books and a nice back yard. There's iced tea in the--excuse me, there's Coke and 7 Up in the boxes next to the fridge. When I can come back, we can talk."

Peter relaxed, and he felt better. He told Prof. Johnson. Prof. Johnson said, "That's excellent. What I'd like you to do next is go in to work, with a lawyer I know. You can tell him what's going on, and he'll lead you to a courtroom to observe."

Peter went away to court the next day, and when he came back he was ashen. He said nothing to Prof. Johnson.

Then, after the next day, he came back looking even more unhappy. "The first day, the lawyer, George, took me into divorce court. I thought I saw the worst that divorce court could get. Until I came back today. It was the same--this sickening scene where two people had become the most bitter enemies. I hope it doesn't come to this. This was atrocious. It was vile. It was more than vile. It was--"

Prof. Johnson sent him back for a third day. This time Peter said nothing besides, "I think I've been making a mistake."

After the fourth day, Peter said, "Help me! I've been making the biggest mistake of my *life*!"

After a full week had passed, Peter said, "*Please*, I *beg* you, don't send me back there."

Prof. Johnson sent Peter back to watch a divorce court for one more miserable, excruciating day. Then he said, "Now you can do whatever you want. What do you want to do?"

The conflict between Peter and Mary ended the next day.

Peter went home, begging Mary for forgiveness, and no sooner than he had begun his apology, a thousand things were reflected in Mary's face and she begged his forgiveness. Then they talked, and debated whether to go back to Wheaton, or stay where they were. Finally Mary said, "I really want to go back to Wheaton."

Peter began to shyly approach old friends. He later misquoted: "I came crawling with a thimble in the desparate hope that they'd give a few tiny drops of friendship and love. Had I known how they would respond, I would have come running with a bucket!"

Peter and Mary lived together for many years; they had many children and were supported by many friends.

Ployon said, "I didn't follow every detail, but... there was something in that that stuck."

Archon said, "How long do you think it lasted?"

"A little shorter than the other one, I mean first part."

"Do you have any idea how many days were in each part?"

"About the same? I assume the planet had slowed down so that a year and a day were of roughly equal length."

"The first part took place during three days. The latter part spanned several thousand days--"

"I guess I didn't understand it--"

"--which is... a sign that you understood something quite significant... that you knew what to pay attention to and were paying attention to the right thing."

"But I didn't understand it. I had a sense that it was broken off before the end, and that was the end, right?"

Archon hesitated, and said, "There's more, but I'd rather not go into that."

Ployon said, "Are you sure?"

"You won't like it."

"Please."

The years passed and Peter and Mary grew into a blissfully happy marriage. Mary came to have increasing health problems as a result of the accident, and those around them were amazed at how their love had transformed the suffering the accident created in both of their lives. At least those who knew them best saw the transformation. There were many others who could only see their happiness as a mirage.

As the years passed, Jacob grew to be a good friend. And when Peter began to be concerned that his wife might be... Jacob had also grown wealthy, very wealthy, and assembled a top-flight legal team (without taking a dime of Peter's money--over Peter's protests!), to prevent what the doctors would normally do in such a case, given recent shifts in the medical system.

And then Mary's health grew worse, much worse, and her suffering grew worse with it, and pain medications seemed to be having less and less effect. Those who didn't know Mary were astonished that someone in so much pain could enjoy life so much, nor the hours they spent gazing into each other's eyes, holding hands, when Mary's pain seemed to vanish. A second medical opinion, and a third, and a fourth, confirmed that Mary had little chance of recovery even to her more recent state. And whatever measures been taken, whatever testimony Peter and Mary could give about the joy of their lives, the court's decision still came:

The court wishes to briefly review the facts of the case. Subject is suffering increasingly severe effects from an injury that curtailed her life greatly as a young person. from which she has never recovered, and is causing increasingly complications now that she will never again have youth's ability to heal. No fewer than four medical opinions admitted as expert testimony substantially agree that subject is in extraordinary and excruciating pain; that said excruciating pain is increasing; that said excruciating pain is increasingly unresponsive to medication; that subject has fully lost autonomy and is dependent on her husband; that this dependence is profound, without choice, and causes her husband to be dependent without choice on others and exercise little autonomy; and the prognosis is only of progressively worse deterioration and increase in pain, with no question of recovery.

The court finds it entirely understandable that the subject, who has gone through such trauma, and is suffering increasingly severe complications, would be in a state of some denial. Although a number of positions could be taken, the court also finds it understandable that a husband would try to maintain a hold on what cannot exist, and needlessly prolong his wife's suffering. It is not, however, the court's position to judge whether this is selfish...

For all the impressive-sounding arguments that have been mounted, the court cannot accord a traumatized patient or her ostensibly well-meaning husband a privelege that the court itself does not claim. The court does not find that it has an interest in allowing this woman to continue in her severe and worsening state of suffering.

Peter was at her side, holding her hand and looking into his wife's eyes, The hospital doctor had come. Then Peter said, "I love you," and Mary said, "I love you," and they kissed.

Mary's kiss was still burning on Peter's lips when two nurses hooked Mary up to an IV and injected her with 5000 milligrams of sodium thiopental, then a saline flush followed by 100 milligrams of pancurium bromide, then a saline flush and 20 milligrams of potassium chloride.

A year later to the day, Peter died of a broken heart.

Ployon was silent for a long time, and Archon was silent for an even longer time. Ployon said, "I guess part of our world is present in that world. Is that what you mean by being in two places at once?"

Archon was silent for a long time.

Ployon said, "It seems that that world's problems and failings are somehow greater than our achievements. I wish that world could exist, and that we could somehow visit it."

Archon said, "Do you envy them that much?"

Ployon said, "Yes. We envy them as--"

Archon said, "--as--" and searched through his world's images.

Ployon said, "--as that world's eunuchs envy men."
Archon was silent.
Ployon was silent.

www.ingramcontent.com/pod-product-compliance
Lightning Source LLC
Chambersburg PA
CBHW030814310726
48980CB00006B/498/J
9780615202174